The Nordman

Catherine Birch grew up in Leicestershire in the Midlands. She has always had a passion for horses and animals. At eighteen she bought her first horse and now has two horses, Pampas and Freedom. She also has four cats and a tortoise.

Catherine's interests include ultra-marathons. She has competed in many six day self-sufficiency races across the deserts of the world to raise money for charity including the infamous Marathon des Sables in 2007 and 2010. In 2012 Catherine rode her bike from Land's End to John O'Groats also for charity.

Catherine Birch

The Nordman

Cover Illustration by Harriat King

Olympia Publishers
London

www.olympiapublishers.com

OLYMPIA PAPERBACK EDITION

A CIP catalogue record for this title is
available from the British Library.

ISBN: 978-1-84897-791-4

This is a work of fiction.
Names, characters, places and incidents originate from the writer's
imagination. Any resemblance to actual persons, living or dead, is purely
coincidental.

First Published in 2016

Olympia Publishers
60 Cannon Street
London
EC4N 6NP
Printed in Great Britain

Dedication

To those who know, with great power comes great
responsibility

Acknowledgments

From a very young age I was told I had an overactive imagination. Unfortunately, being unable to channel my imagination into anything constructive often landed me in trouble. My position at a large high street retailer enabled me to meet Mr Dave Brown of Dave Brown Christmas Trees, whose incredible knowledge and passion for his subject inspired me to write this book. I would like to thank him for (temporarily) diverting my imagination along a constructive and very enjoyable route and for helping me with some of the finer points of Christmas tree production.

Having worked for the same company for twenty-six years, I have a lot of friends who, in whatever way, large or small, have given me incredible support and encouraged me to get *The Nordman* published. I thank them all from the bottom of my heart and hope they enjoy the story.

To define my IT skills as basic would be polite to say the least. The times I have had to call downstairs from my back bedroom office (often in the middle of a life changing rugby match) for help are without number so I have to say a very big thank you to my IT support analyst and husband Chris Birch.

Chapter One

The cold wind felt refreshing as it blew against Tori's hot face. Her horse beneath her was galloping hard and she breathed in the smell his sweat, mixed along with the aroma of autumnal decaying leaves from the forest floor. Flecks of sweat were all over her jodhpurs and riding boots, mixed together with mud churned up from the horse's flying hooves. The forest floor sounded hollow beneath Carlos' huge hooves as they made light work of the hill side ahead of them. She urged him onwards up the hill toward the top. She smiled to herself, taking in the enjoyment of riding her horse and her picturesque surroundings. Slowing to a canter and then a trot and walk, she let her horse have a long rein and stretch his neck. He was a fit horse and it didn't take him long to get his breath back from the gallop. Carlos had been a big part of Tori's life for many years; he was her rock, her place of solitude and resolve. She remembered a time when he was a nervous, lanky four-year-old, afraid of his own shadow. Her brother Tim had rescued him and given him to her as a twenty-first birthday present. She would be forever grateful to him for bringing them together.

Carlos' large, well-shod hooves clattered onto the cobbles of the stable yard as they arrived back. Tori loosened Carlos' girth and swung her leg over the back of the saddle, dismounting onto the cobbles of the yard. She attached Carlos' head collar to a ring in the wall outside his stable with a quick release knot should he decide to pull back suddenly. Carefully, she removed his saddle and bridle and groomed the dried sweat and mud from him. His muscles twitched as she moved the body brush over him. She pushed down hard, moving the brush over his taut body to remove the ingrained mud, then she ran it over the metal curry comb in her left hand, cleaning the brush as she went. He turned his head toward her and grasped the edge of her pocket and tugged hard. He was looking for treats, she laughed at his behaviour and handed some to him. He gently took them from her hand with his lips tickling her with his long whiskers. Leading him into his large and well-bedded down stable, she fetched his dinner from the feed room next door, tipping it into his feed bucket inside his stable and standing back to watch as Carlos tucked into it without hesitation. He scraped a huge hoof along the stable floor, flicking up straw as it went. He was hungry after his ride. He was an amazing horse, at 17.1 hands high he was vast. He was flaxen chestnut in colour, having a golden coat with almost white mane and tail. He had two white socks on his front legs and a white blaze running down the middle of his face. He had transformed in the eleven years he had lived with her into a kind and generous horse who would face anything with her on board. She would have the time to enjoy being with him now she was here for six months.

Finishing up, she hung his hay net and then dressed him in his stable rug, ready for the night. Carefully closing the door, she went into the tack room to hang up the saddle and bridle rinsing the bit in the sink and quickly removing the mud off the girth on the saddle. She chatted casually to the staff who were enjoying coffee in the tack room about their Christmas plans. It was, after all, only just around the corner. She thought about the gifts she must get sorted out for her friends and family back home.

Driving back to the cottage she was renting, in her battered old Volkswagen, Tori's thoughts returned to Nick. They had been together for five years and had almost gotten married when she had caught him in bed with his very young PA. That had been the end of it for Tori and she had packed her bags and left him. Despite the calls and text messages from him begging her to go back, she knew that this was the right decision. He had been the love of her life and she had been devastated by his actions. After weeks of deliberating, she had decided to move away and had rented the cottage in the Herefordshire countryside for six months to get herself together. She would decide what to do next once she had recovered herself.

The large, metal key turned in the old oak door and Tori let herself into the old cottage, locking up behind her. The cottage was built of stone and had low ceilings. The oak front door led into a small hallway with a coat cupboard to the right. The flagstone floor led into a kitchen/dining room on the left hand side and a fair sized lounge on the right with a large fireplace. The stairs from the hallway led up to the two bedrooms and bathroom upstairs. The smell of the open fire still filled the small cottage, it was warm from the night before. She smiled, this cottage was a real find, a holiday rental that now out of season, she had managed to get for next to nothing to rent for the six months. She had found it online one day. 'A stone's throw away from the picturesque village of Great Diameade', the web site had told her. Indeed the village was very picturesque, filled with beautiful cottages not unlike the one she was renting and houses built out of the local sandstone, her new setting was very beautiful. It was certainly very uplifting to move somewhere so beautiful in the middle of winter.

Moving into the small kitchen, she opened the fridge and got out a bottle of wine. She then put herself a supermarket pizza into the oven and went to run a bath.

As she lowered herself into the thick crust of bubbles, she took a sip out of the wine. It was cold and tasted good. Elderflower, her favourite wine. She dared herself to hope things would get better for her one day. She knew that day was still a long way off. The first six months after the break up with Nick, she had not been able to see further than the bottom of the next wine bottle. She had given up running and going to work had been unbearable – all the questions people asked her and trying not to think of Nick all the time and forever questioning herself. Wedding arrangements had had to be cancelled. Invitations had gone out and she had had to call everyone and tell them that the wedding was off and explain why. She still had her wedding dress hanging up at home.

Her mother thought she should have given Nick a second chance but how would she ever be able to trust him again after that ultimate betrayal? She had later found out that the affair had been going on for over a year and she had been totally oblivious. The bottom had dropped out of her world. How could she have been so wrong about someone, someone that she was only weeks away from marrying and had wanted to have a family with? That was what had made her decide to take a six month break from work and move away and try to make a fresh start. Her manager at the florist shop had been brilliant with her and had agreed to give her full pay for the time she was away. That had been eight weeks ago now. She found it hard to imagine she had not been here longer.

Later, she sat alone at the table in the kitchen she crunched on the crust of the pizza and thought of her ride in the forest. She was so glad that she had kept Carlos fit and had brought him with her to Herefordshire. It had been so hard in the early days, dragging herself out every day to come and ride him, suffering from terrible hangovers and being deeply depressed. She thought of the days she had ridden him with tears streaming down her face, she remembered those only too well. Still, she would have been in a much worse place if she had not had Carlos to run to. She had always come back from her rides in a better frame of mind and it had been on one of those rides when she had made the decision to move away, leave it all behind and take on a new life, if only for a few months.

Tori had never lived anywhere other than her home in Leicestershire. She had loved living there until it had turned into her own personal prison. She knew too many people, both friends and customers in the shop. She had realised she would never get any better if she stayed. She had decided to move to Herefordshire because she had once seen it on TV and thought how nice it looked. It had not taken her long to find somewhere on the internet and the following week she was moving in.

Waking early as she always did, Tori showered and ate a breakfast of yogurt and fruit before pulling on her riding clothes and her now clean boots and driving her way back to the stables.

Carlos whinnied to her as she pulled up. He knew the sound of her car and was already pacing around his stable, wanting his hay. Tori put in a net of hay and started with the mucking out, piling heaps of manure and wet straw into the wheelbarrow and then taking it over to the stables muck heap for rotting down. Once finished, she removed Carlos' rug and groomed him with the soft bristled body brush, carefully removing any dust and muck from his gold, glossy coat whilst he munched on his hay net. After his groom, Tori fetched his saddle and bridle and tacked him up. Carlos was prancing around when she lead him out of his stable, excited about the impending ride, but she managed to leap on board from the mounting block and tighten his girth before reaching the gate to the road.

A mile or so along the road was the turn into the forest. Tori loved this route, the smell of the leaves and the pine needles, the sound of Carlos' pounding hooves on the earth as they moved along, ducking under the low branches. Carlos was thoroughly warmed up after his trot along the road and started to snort and snatch at his bit wanting to go faster. His breath plumed out of his flaring nostrils but she would not let him go yet, not until they were well out of the reach of the low branches. At the bottom of the hill Carlos sprang into a controlled and bouncy canter, his long legs eating up the earth beneath them. She felt like she could take on the world when she was on his back, he was an equine powerhouse full of muscle, strength and prowess.

The hill took a good few minutes to ride up of which Carlos brought himself back to a trot and then a walk. This was the same route she had taken yesterday afternoon. Today she decided to make it slightly longer with a ride around to the further side of the forest. Taking up her reins and nudging Carlos back into a trot they took the left fork in the bridle path and made their way into unknown territory. Passing woody clearings and a few startled squirrels collecting their winter nuts, she realised that life was at that moment starting to feel good again.

Chapter Two

One swift motion of the chainsaw and the old tree fell to the ground, shaking and casting its leaves in its wake. The man responsible for the demise of the old tree wiped the sweat from his brow with the sleeve of his old black fleece and took a minute to gain his breath. Over in the distance he watched the woman canter her horse up the hill side. A fabulous massive creature with a flowing mane and tail that looked almost ethereal. The woman on board was slim, her long ponytail flew out behind her as she rode the horse up the hill and off into the distance.

Starting his chainsaw again, Johan cut the old oak into chunks for the fire and tossed them effortlessly into the back of his pickup. It was nearly dark by the time he had driven across the forest and back home along the twisting old forest track, navigating the pot holes and lumps that had appeared in the road over the last thirty five years he had driven it. Unloading the logs, he carried a few of the smaller ones inside and thrust them into his Aga. Wiping his large rugged hands on his weathered jeans, he went upstairs to shower. Rinsing the suds from his strong yet aging body, he stood under the stream of hot water, thinking about the woman on the horse and wondering who she was.

Sleep came easily to the man who worked the forest and he awoke early from a dreamless sleep. Dressing in an old T-shirt and even older Levis, he contemplated the day ahead as he ate his porridge and drank a mug of steaming tea. He had a couple more of the old oak trees to maintain as some branches had come down in the last storm. He would be on the far side of the forest and away from the bridle path so would not be seeing the woman with the horse if she came back that way. Packing his lunch and Thermos, he clambered into the battered pickup and started off to the far side of the forest some three miles away.

Living alone had not been something Johan had chosen but in his type of work it was hard to meet people, and living on the outskirts of the forest was not really the place to meet people. He had been alone for twenty years now since Tabatha had decided New York was the place to live and not Herefordshire. He had been immensely sad when she had left but he bore her no malice. Forest life was not for everyone and he had worried when she moved into his house that she would not enjoy the outdoor life. He had never met anyone else and had resigned himself to a solitary life.

Johan's Norwegian father, Hans, had trained him in forestry, he had started the Christmas tree plantation that now belonged to Johan. After Johan's mother Ingrid had passed away, leaving them alone to cope, they carried on managing the forest and plantation together. His father had long gone now, leaving him alone most of the time, unless friends or colleagues decided to pop by and share some banter with the aging forester.

Bouncing around in the pickup along the tracks he had driven for what seemed like forever, Johan came to a prompt stop when he saw branches on the ground. This part of the forest was a public footpath and needed to be maintained or the council would be getting onto the forestry society about it. Johan's close friend and sometimes colleague was already assessing the damage and commented as he was taking the chainsaw out of the back of the truck. "Looks like we will need to get these branches moved pretty quickly," said Angus. "I think the weather is going to change tonight and we might not get another chance." Angus was a much smaller and very grey haired slim man, Johan's long-time friend who often shared a whisky on special occasions and often invited him to share a meal with his wife and himself. He was considerably older than Johan and had known his father so felt he was to look after and advise him.

The men worked for several hours together with chainsaws and smaller handsaws to move and chop the wood, loading it into their vehicles as they worked. They chatted as they worked, enjoying each other's company. It was late November and the weather had promised a few days of rain and then it was to start getting cold, so finishing the job today would be the best.

It had turned dusk and they were just finishing up their work. Johan's thoughts were on the woman with the horse and he asked Angus if he knew anything about her, she had been plaguing his thoughts. "I have never seen her before but I have seen her riding the bridleway six times in the last eight weeks, do you know who she is or where she is from?" he asked him. Angus replied he didn't but she might be someone from the stables a few miles away hiring a horse whilst on holiday.

Driving back to his cottage, trying his best to navigate the ruts and bumps in the track, Johan hoped the horse woman wasn't a temporary fixture. She was someone he decided he wanted to meet.

Chapter Three

Carlos had been lame for a couple of days now. Whilst out in the field he had cast a shoe and then spent the afternoon running around and made himself foot-sore. Tori finished picking out his feet and hung his hay up. He was spending the next few days in his stable to make sure he didn't do any more damage to himself. Carlos was not pleased about the fact so Tori quickly exited the stable before he could try and barge out after her. She had decided to spend the morning catching up on her emails and calls back home to her family, something she was not looking forward to as she was sure to get a lecture from her mother regarding Nick.

Running the four miles back to the cottage, Tori stopped at the small village shop to collect a few groceries. The shop keeper was always friendly towards her and enquired as to how she was getting along in the cottage. "I really love it there," Tori told him. "It is the best thing that I could ever have done, move out here with my horse." The shop keeper handed over her groceries and as she packed them into her small backpack he responded, smiling. "Well, you certainly moved here at the right time, we are due for a bit of bad weather, I hope that you have enough wood to keep you warm for a few days?" She assured him that she did and if she was running low she would let him know. He told her the number for the wood supplier was in the top drawer by the telephone table in her cottage.

After loading the groceries into the kitchen cupboards, Tori checked the drawer by the phone table. She found the number scribbled on a piece of paper titled *wood man, give two days' notice*. Secretly smiling to herself, she wondered who the *wood man* was and why he would need to have two days' notice.

Tori didn't relish the task of calling back home to see how her family were. She knew her mother would give her a lecture and that is what happened.

"Nick has called and wants to meet up with you, why won't you give him a second chance?" her mother snapped down the telephone. "He is really sorry and you know you will not find another catch like him in a hurry?"

Wow, didn't she know it. Who would want to catch their fiancé in bed with another woman at any stage in their relationship? Her mother was of the old school and just couldn't understand Tori's response. "Mother, I would rather be on my own for the rest of my life than always be wondering where he was, who he was with if he was late home, I just cannot understand why you cannot see that." She knew she was beating her head against a brick wall and the call ended when her mother again had a go at her.

"And why will you not let me have your phone number at the cottage or address? Nobody has any idea where you are and couldn't contact you if anything was to happen to any of us." Little did her mother realise that Tori knew who would be knocking on her door if she did give her number or address to anyone apart from her brother Tim.

She ended the call, cross with herself and stressed. Speaking with her mother always had that effect on her and she hated the fact that she did have to call every week or so to check in on home. Tori's father had passed away many years ago now, he had been taken by a swift heart attack. One day here and then he was gone. Her mother had turned into a real bother without her father there to keep her in check and Tori bore the brunt of her bad moods.

It had been her brother Tim who had told her to go and not give her number or address out, he knew his mother only too well. Still, she would speak with him later when he was back from work. Tim had been brilliant after the break up and had driven her and Carlos down to the cottage. Sworn to secrecy, he was the only one who knew where Tori was hiding out. She knew he wouldn't let her secret out to anyone.

After an hour on her laptop, Tori had a break and made herself a cup of tea and fetched in more wood for the fire. Throwing on two large logs, the fire hissed and spat as it sprang back into life. She looked out of the window and realised that the weather was turning for the worse. She could see the rain starting on the window of her car and the sky was grey, promising that it would be here for a while.

Tori checked on Carlos later that afternoon. He seemed more settled now so she quickly skipped him out and then removed his rugs and gave him a thorough grooming. Removing all the bedding that had gotten tangled into his mane and tail, she sponged his eyes and nostrils to freshen him up. After giving his hooves a coat of hoof oil, she fetched his dinner from the feed room. There was nobody in the feed room to chat with. She remembered that all the staff were on a half day to go and buy Christmas presents. Something she had spent most of the morning doing on her laptop, all for gift wrapping and sending straight to her family from the store. She was not planning any impromptu visits home over Christmas. She was planning to spend it in the cottage alone.

Finishing up with Carlos, Tori put him his night rug on, making sure it was well fastened at the front and under his tummy. Sometimes she had found he could get out of his rug and it was too cold for that now. She hung his night hay net and refilled his water bucket. Closing his stable door behind her, she made her way back to her car. The weather was horrendous and as she drove back to the cottage she had to turn the wipers on full and slow right down so she didn't miss the well-hidden turn. Bumping along the road to the cottage, she tried to be careful to miss the pot holes but that was not an easy task. Really she would have been better to have borrowed Tim's four wheel drive and let him have her car until she returned. Still, Tim needed it for his horses too. She cursed herself for not asking him if she could use it here.

Back at the cottage, the fire was still in action so Tori loaded it back up and went to have a bath. Relaxing in the bubbles, she called Tim to find out how he was. It was so good to talk to him. She hoped that he would suggest a visit down to see her over Christmas but he said he couldn't due to not having much time off and having to spend it with their mother. "You know what she is like," he said, "all she wants to know is where you are and if I can persuade you to come back and marry Nick, she just won't listen." Poor Tim, he had sacrificed so much since Tori had moved. "How are you getting on with that crazy horse these days?" he asked her, referring to Carlos as he once was.

"He is brilliant," she told him. "We have been out riding most days and have found a great bridle path through the forest which we have been doing a few times. I have decided to give Carlos a rest from all the schooling that we used to do when we didn't really have good riding country." Tim promised to visit when he could and work would permit.

Chapter Four

The rain was lashing against Johan's window in his house, streaming down the windows in small rivers. Looking outside at the downpour, he had decided that today would be spent doing paperwork and then he would cut up some wood in his large barn. There were a few large trunks that needed to be chopped up ready for the winter which now looked as though it had arrived. Turning away from the view out of the window, he put on the kettle and started to make himself a mug of tea, dragging out the half-full cake tin at the same time. He thought to himself that being self-employed did sometimes have its benefits.

Ringing around various suppliers, he paid up a few of his invoices for fuel and a new chain for his chainsaw. He had also bought some specialist clothing he had to wear for his job. He sighed at how much things cost, not that he couldn't afford it; his parents had been very careful with money and had left him well provided for. He didn't see the point of spending unless he had to but he didn't buy second best either. His chainsaw was top of the range Stihl and his protective clothes were of the same make.

He made a trip into the village in his truck to collect some odd bits of shopping from the grocery shop. Loading the gravy granules, potatoes, sugar and shower gel onto the counter, Johan made sure that he told the shop keeper to pass on the message to the landlords of the holiday rentals. He would be making wood deliveries in the next week, if anyone would like some to let him know. Johan was a very well-liked member of the community and the shop keeper assured him that he would pass on the message. He told him he had already checked with one of the holiday rentals and she was aware of his services. Johan had provided the village with a large amount of Christmas trees that year and they had all sold. He was due to send extra ones in the next week or so but standing proudly outside the shop by the war memorial was one of Johan's prize Nordman firs. He smiled as he closed the shop door behind him, catching sight of the huge tree.

That afternoon he made himself busy with his Stihl chainsaw, cutting up logs into firewood sizes and then stacking them in the far side of his barn. Later he cut up the large chunks of wood with a log splitter to break into smaller pieces suitable for smaller fires and wood burning stoves. He loved the task of cutting the wood, he found it relaxing and gave him time to think. He stripped his shirt off and removed his protective trousers as it was warm work. Johan was a large framed man, of well over six feet. He had an extremely muscular physique and at fifty-two years old, he sported a thick grey mop of hair which was cut into a crew cut most of the time. Lately though, it looked messy. Although he did look older than his fifty-two years, his body was amazingly well toned and could have been that of a forty year old. Sweat from his effort had started to run down his chest, trickling through the matted grey hairs and down to the top of his jeans as he swung the splitter that had belonged to his father. Stopping briefly to wipe his forehead with his shirt, he realised that he had been chopping and sawing all afternoon and it had started to get dark.

The rain had started to cease as Johan stacked the last of the wood in the corner of the barn. He picked up his protective trousers and shirt from the work bench and walked back to his house, locking the barn and all his kit inside. Even though it was remote out here, he didn't want to chance being burgled. Hanging the log splitter up inside his house, he put his shirt back on and made himself a mug of tea, taking a piece of cake from the tin that Angus' wife had delivered to him. The thick fruit cake was fabulous and rich. There was more than a hint of alcohol and he devoured the piece without leaving a crumb. He thought of Angus' wife Mary, she was a lovely woman. She had taken Johan under her wing when his father had passed away and since had taken it upon herself to provide him with cakes on a weekly basis, not that he was complaining, it was a nice thing to have someone worrying about him and caring. She had often tried to get him out on dates with local women but Johan wasn't interested. Mary had now decided that if he wanted a woman he would go out and find one himself.

Finishing the last bit of cake and downing the dregs from his mug of tea, Johan rang around to make sure his clients knew he was making the wood deliveries the following day. He did know one of the holiday cottages was rented out at the moment and if he should just pop by on the off chance to see if they wanted wood. He wasn't sure if the landlord had left his number and the weather was due to turn very cold. He would see how he went for time and decide on the day. He had to make a delivery to the manor house up the road, which would mean he would have to take his trailer as they had fires and wood burning stoves to fill. He would make that delivery first and then come back and load the pickup with the next lot.

The rain had started again when he sat down later to his dinner, a single dinner for one. Johan was a good cook, thankfully, as he had a massive appetite. Keeping his huge muscle bound body fed was no easy task. Tearing at the steak on his plate, his thoughts turned again to the woman with the horse. He decided that tomorrow on his wood delivery rounds he would ask around and see if anyone knew who she was. That decision made he finished up his meal and went to shower.

The next morning, it had stopped raining but instead it was about ten degrees colder than of late. Johan loaded up the trailer and his pickup and made his way to the manor house that was three miles up the road from his cottage. Arriving there, he was met by the gardener. "Hi there, Johan, I wasn't sure what day you were coming this week 'cos of the weather," he shouted across to him.

"I decided to come today because I am not sure if I will have to make more deliveries due to the holiday lets, not sure if they are empty now or not and I am waiting for a call from the landlord," Johan shouted back to him. "I did call yesterday to let you know I was coming, did they not pass the message onto you from the office?" He enquired. The gardener, Michael, had fetched a wheelbarrow to help Johan unload the wood into the various stores around the house.

"Not sure but I had heard that one of the cottages is let out for a six month let at the moment so there is at least one person up there," Michael added. "If the cold is coming then they will surely need a good store of wood in case they get snowed in or something." He was sounding concerned to Johan, so he decided he surely would call the landlord if he didn't have time to stop by on his rounds today.

Next stop was at an old retired couple's house on the outskirts of the manor. They had both worked at the manor when they had been younger and had met and married whilst serving there. The owner of the manor had given them the cottage for their long service and loyalty. He didn't provide the wood though but they always paid on delivery and gave Johan a cup of tea into the deal. Johan also had a small potted tree in the back of his truck for them. He took it out tapping the bottom of the pot onto the floor to remove the dead needles that had congregated inside the tree.

After the second delivery, Johan went back to his house to load his pickup again. Bouncing around over the very poorly maintained forest tracks Johan made his way to collect Angus. On his way back out to the road, they drove to their furthest delivery which was ten miles out of the village to a smallholding owned by a young couple with two small children. Johan and Angus unloaded the wood into their wood store, carefully stacking it at the back so to fill the whole store. They stopped to chat with them for a while and look at a couple of rare breed sheep they had recently bought. The couple seemed to be doing really well since they had arrived two years ago. The smallholding had been derelict and they had lived in a caravan for most of the two years, until the work had been completed, and now they had moved into the house before the winter started.

On the way back, Angus asked Johan to stop by his house as they needed some wood too. "Mary has been going on about the weather changing and is nagging me to get the wood in before the snow and ice comes," Angus reported. Johan always ended up with a massive pile at his house as it was the closest to the forest and had a big barn with all his tools to hand. Angus lived further away so didn't have ready access to the wood. The men loaded the last of the wood into the small shed next to Angus and Mary's kitchen. Mary had been baking bread whilst they had been out and called them in for some lunch – bacon sandwiches on fresh bread, something Johan didn't make for himself and devoured in five minutes.

The afternoon was spent on two further deliveries to a couple of village shops. Johan had told all his deliveries to make sure they gave him two days' notice if they were about to run out so he could make sure he had enough wood chopped and ready to deliver. On the whole, they all kept to this agreement as he was the only person in the area who delivered and unloaded their supply. The village shop keeper had told Johan that there was someone in the holiday cottage and she had told him that she had his number so not to worry, she would be in touch if she needed any wood.

That evening was spent on more boring paperwork, keeping his invoices up to date and incoming and outgoing wood supplies. He realised that he had not mentioned the woman with the horse to anyone today and was cross with himself for forgetting.

Chapter Five

Ten days had passed since Carlos had been lame and he was now back to full health. Tori decided that they would go for a nice sedate hack out in the forest with a small bit of trotting to take the wind out of Carlos' sails. Tacking him up in his stable, she was relieved that she had let him out for a couple of days or he would have been going crazy by now. Presently he seemed happy just to be eating his hay, as she had groomed yesterday's mud from his body.

Outside, she took Carlos to the mounting block and swung her leg over his broad back. Along the road, there was not much traffic and Carlos was happy to walk for the first part and then did a gentle trot. Tori had been talking to the stable staff and had decided to try another route into the forest today. That way Carlos would not get excited and anticipate their canter/gallop hill. She rode past the first track and carried on for another half mile or so down the road. Turning into the field, she rode along the side and made a turn into the forest. She had not been on this side before and the bridle way ran parallel to the road from the stables so she should be okay to make her way back if she got lost. Riding around the edge of the forest, Carlos seemed to be very chilled as they strolled along taking in the cold morning. Without warning a huge pheasant flew up by the side of Carlos startling him badly. Carlos leaped to the left and spun around rearing as the terrified pheasant flew off into the undergrowth. Tori was trying her hardest to stay on but when he reared she fell backwards onto the forest floor with a heavy thump. Carlos didn't hesitate and galloped full pelt off into the forest.

Laying on her back on the floor of the forest Tori opened her eyes. Where was she, what had happened and as she was dressed in riding clothes where was Carlos? Groggily she got to her feet. Her head was spinning and she could feel something running down the side of her face. She touched her face with her fingers and realised that she must have cut herself on something as she had blood on her cheek. She felt for her phone and called the stables to tell them what had happened and had Carlos made his way back at all? She had no idea how long she had been on the forest floor it could have been minutes or hours. Carlos had not arrived back at the stables and they were sending out two people on horses and two in a car to try and find him and her. Tori started to wander into the forest. She wiped at her face as the blood was running down tickling her cheek. She was worried about Carlos, anything could have happened to him, he could have ran out onto the road and been hit by a car. She started to cry at the thought and stumbled onwards through the forest undergrowth.

The huge horse charged into the clearing. His blonde mane and tail flew out behind him like streamers. Johan was working on a young tree and looked up at the creature as he made his entrance. The horse looked terrified, covered in sweat the reins to his bridle were broken and his eyes wide and rolling. He was breathing hard as he came to a stop seeing Johan standing before him. Johan reached out and very slowly took the reins that were hanging down in front of him.

The huge horse tried to spin around and run off but Johan had hold of him. He spoke quietly and soothed the creature. Slowly, he checked him over for any injuries. It seemed that the only thing missing was the rider. On checking the bridle Johan noticed that there was a tag with a number on. Carefully, not wanting to frighten the horse further he reached into his shirt pocket and removed his mobile phone. Calling the number on the tag, there was an answer at the other end. "Mill Bank Stables, James speaking, can I help you?" said the voice on the other end.

"I hope so," replied Johan. "I have hold of a very large ginger horse here who seems to have lost his rider," he told James on the other end of the phone. Realising that the ginger horse was more than likely Carlos, James advised him to walk him to the road where there would be someone with a lorry to bring him back home. The task in hand now would be to find the rider. James asked Johan if he knew which direction the horse had come from, as the rider had taken a new route that day and she was not familiar with the territory and would probably be disorientated by now. Fearing worse from the state of the horse, Johan said he would have a look around the surrounding area before making his way to the road to wait for the lorry to arrive.

Tori walked around for what seemed an age, with tears running down her face. The cut on her face had stopped bleeding now but she was covered in leaves, mud and pine needles. She felt sick and was starting to panic. Rounding the bend in the track that she was on, her heart suddenly pounded hard in her chest. Carlos was walking towards her, being led by a huge strapping man with untidy greying hair. He had the most intense blue eyes she had ever seen and he was smiling at her. She started to cry, so happy now – Carlos was sweaty but looked like he was unharmed by his venture. She started to run towards him and then passed out.

When she came to, she was sitting in the passenger seat of a pickup truck driving on the main road into town. She looked over at the driver and saw it was the same man who had rescued Carlos in the forest. She sat up straight in the seat she asked, "Where are you taking me? I need to sort Carlos out before I go anywhere, where is he?" Johan looked over to her and smiled kindly at her.

"Don't worry, your horse is safely back at the stables. They sent a lorry to fetch him and they said they would sort him out and make sure he was checked every hour through the night. I am taking you to the hospital to get you checked out, you passed out at my feet. Feeling very embarrassed at her rudeness Tori thanked him for looking after Carlos.

"I am so sorry," she explained to him, "It is the first time I rode that route and a pheasant flew up at the side of us and Carlos reared I must have fallen off," she rubbed her cheek, checking the bleeding had stopped. "I am Tori by the way, Tori Brown," she introduced herself.

"Well, Ms Brown," he looked over at her, "I am pleased I could be of service, I am Johan Andersen, at your service. Anytime you should take a tumble in the forest, I quite possibly will be there," he leaned over and shook her grubby hand, smiling at her as he did so.

Arriving at the hospital, Tori told Johan he could leave her there and thanked him for the lift. He told her he would stay and take her back home once they had finished. She was grateful as she had no means of getting home and had not brought any cash with her, apart from the ten pounds she kept in her phone case for emergencies. This was such an emergency but ten pounds would not cover the taxi fare back to the cottage.

Tori was checked over fairly quickly by NHS standards. Johan sat with her the whole time. As she was suffering from a mild concussion and nothing else, they cleaned the cut on her face and discharged her. Johan drove her back to the stables, where he said goodnight and left her to check on Carlos. Once alone, she started to cry again. She could have lost everything today. If Johan had not been in the forest and had not caught hold of Carlos anything could have happened. Most people would have been terrified of a huge, powerful horse covered in sweat and in a big panic. It seemed Johan liked horses and had not been afraid. She was so grateful to him for being their hero.

She drove back to the cottage and poured herself a large whisky to calm her nerves. Slipping out of her clothes and into the shower, she cleansed the mud from her hair and face. Standing under the hot running water, she hoped she would see Johan again to thank him properly when she wasn't covered in mud, blood and tears. She wondered where he lived and if he was married and had children. He must be old enough to be her father but that hadn't stopped a feeling in her heart that he was a good and honourable man and she did want to say thank you properly. Stepping out she quickly dried herself and went to sit by the fireside with her scotch. Sipping out of the large glass, she decided not to tell anyone at home about the incident in the forest. They would only worry about her and she didn't need that at this moment in time. Taking another sip from her glass, she suddenly felt a lot better than she had in a very long time. She hoped that things were starting to look up.

It was three in the morning when Tori woke up on the sofa. The fire had gone out and she was cold. She made her way upstairs to bed. Maybe it had been the shock but she fell asleep straight away once her head was on the pillow. She dreamed of silver pickup trucks and hospital beds, blood and sweaty horses. Waking up at six a.m., she was all hot and breathing heavily. She must have been having a nightmare, something that had not haunted her life since she had moved to Herefordshire.

Chapter Six

Johan woke up and his first thought was Tori. She was the woman he had been thinking of all this time, the woman on the horse – Carlos! He had never expected them to meet in such an unexpected way but now they had met he knew he wanted to keep her in his life. He had never had feelings like this for anyone but he was aware that she would most likely not feel the same way. She had to be at least twenty years his junior and he looked older than he was anyway. She was a beautiful woman of around five feet six inches, slim, with a clear complexion. She was finely proportioned and very muscular. He had wanted to call someone for her to let them know she had suffered a fall but Tori had promptly told him there was nobody to call. Perhaps he was being too perceptive but he didn't believe that statement. Today he decided that he would go and get his hair cut at long last, after he had finished his forestry jobs.

Sawing dead branches with his chainsaw deep in the forest, Johan was being very careful. Hanging thirty feet up in the air by rope, he didn't want any accidents to himself or anyone nearby. Angus had arrived to help him and had already heard about the events of the afternoon before, but wanted to hear the full 'true' version not the one going about in the village. He relayed the story as he scaled the huge tree in the mostly oak forest and relieved it of the dead and dangerous branches. The Stihl chainsaw growled on tick over as the branch hit the forest floor. Turning it off, Johan moved higher up the tree to tackle another branch that had to come down. The rain they had received in recent weeks was not making his job any easier as the trunk was very wet. He dug his crampons into the trunk and revved the Stihl back into life. The branch was down in a couple of minutes and Johan made his way back to the ground. Removing his helmet and visor and running his fingers through his greying mop, he returned the kit to the back of his pickup. Angus had already started to cut the branches into smaller pieces and they both loaded them into Johan's truck.

They worked on through the afternoon around the forest, maintaining a few of the trees and making runs back to Johan's barn with the wood to dry out and be cut into logs. As dusk arrived they parted and Johan went inside. He thought about Tori, wondering where she was staying. He hadn't had a chance to find out and it would look mighty suspicious if he turned up at the stable yard. He resigned himself to the fact that he would probably only see her again if she rode the bridle way, secretly hoping she would. Before his supper, he drove into the village and had a haircut. The barber had heard of the accident with Tori too. The apparent source of the gossip had come from the head lad at the stables – James. James was dating the barber, who it seemed had told just about everyone in the village! Johan decided to take the opportunity to find out where Tori was staying. The barber didn't know and nor did James it seemed, he only had her phone number and Tori had only moved to the area a couple of months previously. There was some angst about a previous relationship that she was wanting to escape but nobody knew if she was a permanent fixture in the village or not. Johan paid the barber, got back into his pickup and drove back to his house. What was going to be his next plan?

The following morning it was raining again and very cold. Johan decided that he would visit the plantation and deliver a few more of the trees that he had cut down a few days previous. He needed to net them, something he couldn't do until they had been cut a day or so in case they went into shock and stayed with their branches upturned as they were netted up. He had at least another twenty to get out to the shops in the village. It seemed this year the trend was live Christmas trees. He also planned to cut up some of the wood that they collected yesterday and hopefully the rain would pass by in the afternoon. He dressed in a plaid shirt and jeans, which would be fine for the job in hand. He wasn't going to be using the Stihl today, only the log splitter, so he didn't need protective gear. Lacing up his steel toecap boots, he walked out into the morning.

Outside, the temperature had taken a very big drop. The rain was more like sleet now and Johan could see his breath pluming out in front of him. Pulling his shirt a little closer to his chest, he hurried to his truck and drove to his plantation. It wasn't a vast size but it was well looked after and the trees were a good quality of which he prided himself. He netted them up without much effort and carefully put them into the back of his truck, and the trailer he remembered to hitch up at the last moment. He delivered to three shops in the village all of who were very pleased to have them. "We ran out mid last week," he was told by the DIY counter staff. "They have been asking us as it seems nobody has any left already," they told him. That was good news, it meant he wouldn't have to collect any back to dispose of.

That afternoon he went into the barn with the log splitter. He fetched a pile of the logs and started working on them quickly to warm up. It didn't take long for him to get warm as he swung the splitter over his head and down into each huge piece of wood, sending the split pieces all over the floor. After a couple of hours working, he went back inside and made a coffee. Hugging the cup against his large, calloused hands, he shivered and decided that it was time the winter clothes came out, another job on his list. He finished the cake Mary had made and washed out the tin, placing it on the draining board for returning. He hoped she would refill the tin with another one of her delicious creations.

Angus called to say that there had been more delivery requests that morning as people were starting to panic over the bad weather. Loading the truck with wood this time Johan drove to Angus with the empty tin and collected him from his doorstep. Turning the heater up to full blast, Angus commented, "By God it has gotten cold. I knew it would arrive soon so we had best get prepared with the wood." Johan assured him that he had spent most of the morning delivering trees and cutting up and storing what they already had from the forest and had another pile from further around that had been brought in by the foresters working the far side of the forest, as they didn't have storage for it.

Arriving at the manor house, they both got out of the truck to unload. Michael greeted them with a wheelbarrow and they promptly filled it and went to fetch a second one. Filling up the various stores at the manor house took quite a while but between the three of them, two wheelbarrows and good banter, the time passed quickly. Waving goodbye to Michael, they went onto the smallholding and a couple of shops in the village. It was three weeks until Christmas and already people had their decorations out and some trees up. Johan was beginning to feel festive especially now the cold weather had arrived. He decided to himself that he would look out a suitable tree in the plantation for his cottage this year and trying to remember where the old decorations were.

The following morning Johan was back, loading his truck with heaps of fire wood. He had decided that he would keep the truck and trailer loaded now as it was going to be more likely that people would be wanting emergency wood deliveries with it being cold. The forecast had said that they would be getting some snow.

Johan was in his barn and had spent several hours doing well needed maintenance on his machinery. He had dropped off his spare Stihl saw for a service and had been checking blades and chains on various other bits. His phone started to ring – it was Angus. "Mate, we have really got to get the truck out, it seems that everyone has heard that we may get snow and have four more deliveries to make today. Can you come and pick me up in about half hour?" Johan sighed, it always went like this in the winter, everyone decided to panic buy.

"Yeah sure, I will just lock up here and then I'll be over to collect you, make sure you are ready."

Hanging up his kit, he locked up the barn after himself and reached into his pocket for the keys to the truck.

Angus was ready, holding a tin of Mary's cake in his hand as Johan pulled up to collect him. He passed it over to Johan, "Mary has been busy in the kitchen this morning and told me to give this to you," was his comment. Johan thanked him and peeped inside at the delicious cakes.

The afternoon deliveries were tedious as everyone they had to deliver to was out. Both men liked to talk to their customers and in this freezing weather they had hoped for a tea at one stop at least but that was not happening today. Quickly, they unloaded the truck, delivery by delivery, and stacked the wood in the relevant shed. The money or cheques were usually left somewhere so Johan would have to spend tomorrow morning on paperwork and a trip to the bank.

Chapter Seven

Tori called the number on the scrap of paper and left a message to say that she was residing at the holiday cottages and had been given this number to call for a wood delivery. She was giving two days' notice but hoped that they could deliver in one day, it was very cold and she wasn't sure she had enough wood left for two days. She was sorry for the short notice. Hanging up, she looked at the scrap of paper and placed it back in the drawer. She hoped that the wood man would pick up her message quickly.

Carlos had been ridden that morning in the sand school at the stables. Tori had decided that he was getting a little bit full of himself, probably due to being in his stable more because of the bad weather churning up the fields. Setting up a course of jumps in the sand school, she had worked him hard, with schooling and then jumping. Carlos was an immensely intelligent horse and she had found that he needed stimulating. Riding that day for two hours had tired herself and Carlos out. She would sleep well that night.

After her ride, she had spent an hour cleaning the saddle and bridle, removing all the sand from the school and the mud that had got ingrained over the last week. Cleaning tack was not Tori's favourite job but she did make a good job of doing it. Running herself a bowl of hot water, she hung the bridle on the hook in the tack room and put the saddle onto the metal saddle horse, removing the girth and stirrups, putting the stirrup irons into another bowl of soapy hot water to clean them. Unbuckling everything on the bridle, she soaked the sponge in the warm water and started to clean the leather thoroughly. After the bridle she did the saddle and stirrup leathers, scrubbing away until they were clean. The girth that held the saddle onto Carlos was last as this was the most dirty item due to the mud and sand that had been flicked up from Carlos' hooves.

After the cleaning, Tori took another sponge and sprayed saddle soap onto it. She loved the rich smell of the soap, it never failed to remind her of ponies at the riding school she had learned to ride at when she was a young girl. Rubbing the soap into the saddle and restoring the shine and suppleness to the leather was something that made all the work worthwhile. She finished up by buckling the bridle back together and threading the stirrup irons back onto the leathers and attaching to the saddle. The girth went over the top of the saddle until she rode again and then she would attach it to the straps.

Collecting the numnah that had been under the saddle and against Carlos' back, she took it to her car to take home and give it a good washing. It had sweat and mud stuck to it, so she found her spare one, fixing that under the saddle for her next ride.

The smell of baking cake was coming out of the Aga, indicating that the lemon drizzle cake she was making would be ready soon. It had been months since she had baked. Fortunately she had found some tins in the bottom of the Aga and had decided to look up online an old recipe she had loved to make – lemon drizzle cake. She stood at the Aga in her jodhpurs, fleece and socks, stirring the lemon juice and sugar to make the drizzle. Realising that she was starting to get back to her old self, she made a note to look up a couple of recipes for Christmas. She loved baking but it was the first thing that had stopped after the break up.

There was a loud knock at the door. Tori removed the drizzle from the top of the Aga and went to answer the door. Opening the old oak door, she was faced with a rather wet Johan.

"Hello," she said, with a big smile spreading across her face. "You had better come inside, you look a bit soggy." She stood back and let him enter.

"Thank you, I think you called and left a message for some wood to be delivered?" he asked. "You have given two days' notice so I hope that you don't mind if we deliver it today. When you called I was driving and we did have some left on the truck."

Realising that Johan was the wood delivery man, Tori was overjoyed. She knew now that she had a way of finding him again "Of course not, come inside and have a warm," she added.

"If you don't mind I will unload the wood first, as it is starting to get dark."

She didn't mind and he knew where to deliver it to, as he often delivered to these cottages. Tori was surprised at herself at how overjoyed she felt at seeing Johan again. What a fool, all these months getting over Nick and now she was having inappropriate feelings for a man old enough to be her father and most probably married or at least involved – you didn't get single men like that one, she decided.

Johan finished up in the wood store and locked the door behind him. He knocked on the cottage door again and Tori lead him inside, where the lemon drizzle was on the side, cooling.

"Would you like tea, I have just made a pot for myself?" she asked.

Sitting down at the large kitchen table, Johan said he would like a cup. She handed him a big mug and sliced off a thick piece of the cake and handed it to him.

"Sorry about the plate," she added, handing him the tin lid. "I can't seem to find any decent ones in the place, should have thought on and brought some with me but I wasn't expecting visitors."

Johan smiled, with a mouthful of the delicious cake trying not to escape his lips, swallowing hard, he said, "They keep the spare plates and things in the attic in a box when the cottages are out of season, do you want me to go up and get them down for you?" he asked.

She said she would if he didn't mind and after a second piece of cake, he fetched the dinner plates, side plates, cups, saucers and bowls down from the attic.

They sat and chatted mostly about Carlos for a while and then Johan said he had to make his way home. Tori thanked him once again for rescuing them and asked him if he knew where she could obtain a Christmas tree from, as she was looking to put up a few festive decorations and had been to the shops in the village and they had all sold out. Johan laughed and said he would get someone to call by with one for her. He left and she felt deflated. Stupid girl, why did she feel like this? She hadn't found anything out about his private life except he worked in the forest and delivered wood. She was cross with herself, she knew she was starting to feel something strong.

Showering that evening, she poured herself another scotch and sat by the fire in her pyjamas. She emailed her mother and told her that she was getting prepared for Christmas. She told her that she had been riding Carlos more and she was fine here and enjoying life more than recently. After, she called Tim. "Hey, sis, how are things with you?" he asked.

She told him that she was starting to feel much better and was looking forward to Christmas, even though she would be on her own here. She loved it at the cottage, he should come down and see it for himself and stop a few days.

Laughing, he replied, "Yeah, I will come and see you sometime, I promise, but mother is being a pain. I told you last time we spoke and we are having her over to stop at Christmas."

Tori felt guilty as it would have been her first Christmas married and she had planned to have her mother to stop with them. She felt a twist of sorrow and guilt in her stomach for all the trouble she had caused everyone over the last months. Hanging up, she returned to her scotch and painful memories.

Chapter Eight

She was out riding the route that she would have done if she had not fallen off Carlos that fateful day. Turning into the forest, she rode along the track, enjoying the fresh air and peacefulness of the forest. There was not a sound to be heard, this was a really quiet route, she thought. She would make sure she came this way again and could possibly use it in her running routes too. Riding on, she passed a Christmas tree plantation. She stopped and looked at all the trees neatly lined up side by side, row after row. They looked like an army of little people, growing into much bigger ones, which must be the trees nearing the end of their life, ones to be chopped down next Christmas. She nudged Carlos on and rode along the track and back onto the road, past her little cottage to the village, making a left turn back to the stables. Carlos was in a lively mood and wanted to jog the whole way round. Tori was cross with him, he needed to get out in the fields more and burn off some of his excess energy, she thought to herself.

At the stables, she rugged Carlos up and turned him out for the afternoon. She had decided that she would spend the evening decorating the tree that had arrived on her doorstep last night. It was a bushy little Nordman fir, one quite possibly out of the forest, probably from the Christmas tree plantation she had passed on her ride earlier. She didn't know who had left it but it must have been someone who Johan had asked. She needed to call him to settle up but she also needed to get more wood delivered. It had snowed briefly that morning and there had been a light covering when she had awoken and opened the curtains in her bedroom.

That afternoon she took herself out for a run in the forest at the back of her house. There was a public footpath that ran through the forest, with a number of tracks she could take. She followed it for a mile or so and then crossed the hill that she and Carlos used to canter up before coming to the main road back to the stables. As she ran she remembered the time when she had stopped running. Once she had been fairly good at marathons and half marathons. Deciding to move on from them, she had taken on ultra-marathons in deserts and had travelled across the world, taking part in six day self-sufficiency ultra-marathons. She had loved racing and meeting new people, she had loved the escapism and the dedication the training had taken and she had loved how she had to push herself way beyond her comfort zone to get the medal at the end of the race. She had raised thousands of pounds for charity and had felt she had been doing something worthwhile. One day she promised herself, there in the middle of the Herefordshire forest, she would return to ultra-marathons, she would once more tackle the Sahara, the Atacama and the Gobi deserts. She didn't want to go back to not running ever again.

She had stopped off at the village shop 'Smiths Hardware' on the way back from the stables and had collected up some decorations and lights that she would use for the little tree. She noticed that they had received a fresh stock of trees since her previous visit. Typical, she thought, but at least now the arrival of her tree meant she would probably see Johan again. Her head full of tree decorations she ran on a little further and then came across a beautiful old house made out of wood. It reminded her of a fairy tale house, it was clad from top to bottom in wood apart from the chimney which was built in the same stone as her cottage. On the side of this house, there was a large wooden barn with big doors. Running on the path toward the house, she saw a truck that she thought was Johan's. Her heart leapt into her mouth when she realised that this must be his house.

She walked around the side of the barn and saw the huge wooden doors were open but before she could go further a voice said, "Well hello, lady, you found me then?" Turning around, she saw him standing in the barn with a huge block of wood in front of him and a wood splitter in his hand. He was stripped off to the waist and sweat was running down his bare chest and stomach; the waistband on his jeans was soaked. Tori stood, gawping at the man before her. Her mouth was open and she couldn't find the words she wanted to say.

She felt like her mouth was full of cotton wool. Okay, he may be old enough to be her father almost but wow, he was some man. His body was vast, with well-toned and very muscular arms and shoulders. He had a band of muscles on his stomach where most men his age would have a beer belly, and just the right amount of greying chest hair. His blue eyes shone out from under his grey hair. She swallowed hard and tried to speak, her mouth opening and shutting and nothing coming out. She felt herself getting very aroused looking at this fabulous man before her and was blushing badly at her inappropriate thoughts and desires.

"Oh, oh er, yes, I am sorry I was out running and I saw your truck, sorry, I didn't mean to disturb you," she mumbled with a reddening, sweaty face.

Johan laughed and reached for his shirt. Walking towards her, she didn't know where to look so she just stared at him. She had never seen anything so overwhelming in her life and was embarrassed but couldn't stop looking at him.

Johan hung up his log splitter and invited her inside his beautiful house. "Did you get the tree I left for you? Was it okay, I didn't ask you what size you wanted?" he asked, looking at her red face.

"Yes," she replied. "It is exactly what I wanted and I need to pay you for it. I am sorry I have been really rude." She was a mess, not knowing where to look and trying not to sound like a stupid little girl!

Johan led her into the kitchen, where he switched on the kettle. "Would you like some tea?" he asked her. "I have some cakes if you would like one of those with your tea." He reached for the tin and handed it to her, whilst he poured the tea out into two large mugs. "You don't owe me anything for the tree," he smiled at her. "Think of it as a welcome to the village for Christmas," he said. "I am putting my tree up today if I can find where I left the decorations the other year." He dunked a large chocolate cake into his tea and she watched as a crumb fell from his lips into his mug.

"You are so kind," she replied. "I feel like I owe you so much already." Her face was starting to return to its natural colour and she reached inside her jacket pocket for a tissue to wipe the sweat away.

"And I need to ask you too if you could do me a repeat wood order for two days," she smiled at him over the top of her mug. "It is getting very cold and I am worried that I will run out of wood. The fire and wood burner seem to eat it," she laughed.

Running back to her chocolate box cottage, brambles grasping at her running tights, she suddenly felt very emotional. She had not started out on her run looking for the forester and had come across him half naked in his barn and it had taken her by surprise. What had taken her more by surprise was how she had felt seeing him like that. She had felt very deep urges and had not felt anything like that for a long time. In fact, she had often thought she would never have sex again after Nick.

From first glance, Johan's house looked like it only had him living there but there had been the cakes obviously home made in a flowery tin so he probably had a girlfriend and not a wife. She should have asked him but didn't feel the time had been right and, really, it was none of her business. The problem was, the more time she was spending with this man, the deeper her feelings were getting.

She knelt down by the tree and carefully started to put the lights on it. The Nordman fir was a prickly customer and she had to push the lights quite far into the tree, because it was bushy and dense. Flicking the switch and satisfied that the lights looked good, she sat back and drew the cord of her dressing gown a little tighter around her. She had just started to hang the baubles when there was a knock on the door. Presuming it was her neighbour returning the lasagne dish he had borrowed, she opened the door.

Standing in front of her was Johan with a cardboard box in his arms. "Hope you don't mind but I found my decorations and remembered that you said you didn't have many for your tree. I have these ones if you would like them?" he added. Looking down at herself, she resigned herself to the fact that yet again he had found her in a mess. This time, though, she was in her dressing gown and pyjamas.

She sighed and opened the door to let him in. "I am so sorry, I would have gotten dressed if I had known you were coming," she said.

"I don't usually slob around in my dressing gown all night, in case you were wondering," she told him, standing with her hands on her hips. He laughed and closed the door behind him.

Standing in the lounge, he admired her work with the lights. "Much better job than mine," he smiled. "These decorations are as old as me and maybe older," he said, handing her the box. "They belonged to my parents and for many years I never put up a tree, but this year I decided things were going to be different so I dug us both a tree from the plantation. Hopefully they will live after Christmas, if you want to keep it." She poured him a scotch and they sat on the floor, adding Johan's baubles to Tori's own, bought that very day from the village hardware store.

That evening Johan told her all she wanted to know, he answered all her questions. He told her he lived alone, he told her about Tabatha and then she told him about Nick and everything that had happened since and why she was living in Herefordshire alone. The evening flew by and they chatted into the early hours of the morning before they realised the time. She waved him off at her door as he took the forest track back to his house in his pickup. She slept very well that night and awoke fresh and ready for the day ahead.

It was a week until Christmas. Tori had written all her cards and sent them from the village post office. All the presents had been purchased online and sent gift wrapped to the recipients. She had ordered her shopping which would be delivered in three days' time to the cottage. She had decided that she was going to invite Johan for dinner before the big day arrived. She had realised that she didn't want to spend the day alone and if he was alone she had planned that she would invite him over then they would have a much better time together. In actual reality, she wanted to see a lot more of him than wood deliveries. That was the story she was telling herself.

She saddled up Carlos and set off on the short ride, feeling very pleased with herself. She nudged him into a trot. He wasn't feeling quite as fresh as he had been yesterday, which was a good thing. They trotted along the road and made the turn into the forest. Carlos was getting excited as the hill was shortly ahead. Tori held him back and then they cantered up the hill. It was a good stretch and by the time they reached the top, Carlos had run out of energy. He was ready to walk before she would normally ask him. She reached down and patted his neck, moving her hand up and down under his thick blonde mane, enjoying the smell of warm horse. They walked the remaining distance back to the stables. Tori groomed him well, removing all tell-tale signs of their ride, and rugged him up in his heavy duty outdoor rug, ready for the afternoon out in the field. He cantered away from the gate as she closed it behind him and down towards the other horses, out enjoying the fresh cold air.

Chapter Nine

Johan had taken a big chance arriving on the doorstep with the old decorations packed up in the box. He didn't know if she would even want them, if they were her style, but she had been so pleased and had told him he was the most thoughtful person she knew! She had offered to return the baubles after she had taken down her tree but he had told her to keep them. When she went back home, he hoped she would put them up at Christmas and think of him. He hadn't been able to believe his luck when she had turned up at his house and been obviously flustered to catch him half naked cutting up wood. He was pleased to see her and her reaction to finding him in the barn. Her face had been red and sweaty from being out running in the cold and she had mud on her shoes and up her running tights but she had looked like a Goddess appearing out of the forest and into his barn. He wondered if she had wanted him as much as he had wanted to take her on the sawdust-covered floor of the barn. Johan was finding desires awakening he had buried for many years.

He had been so lucky to get the tree for her. Driving down to his Christmas tree plantation at the bottom end of the forest, he had found one just the right size. It was marked up on the leader shoot for cutting but he didn't want to cut it, he wanted to dig it up so that if she hung around long enough he could perhaps plant it in her garden or something. He was being emotional, of course she wouldn't hang around. She was probably only here for a few weeks, or at best until after the Christmas break, and then she would be off back to her home. He dug the root ball up and placed it into a large tub, large enough to take all the roots with the soil. Watering it well, he had put it into the back of his truck and taken it around to her house.

He thought of the evening they had spent together. It had been very deep. They had both opened up and discussed their previous relationships. She had told him about her fiancé and the affair he had embarked on. She had told him of her betrayal and dark times that had followed. He had listened to her, resisting the urge to take her in his arms and hold her tight. He had arrived unannounced and caught her in her pink fluffy dressing gown and slippers. Her long blonde hair was flowing over her shoulders and was slightly damp. He had wanted to run his fingers through it and hold her close to him, to tell her it was all going to be all right, but was it? Why would she even feel the same way? He knew she had been hurt and had come to Herefordshire to get over her hurt and heal the wounds. He knew that only her brother knew where she was. At least now he knew why she didn't want him to call anyone after her accident. She wouldn't want to embark on another relationship so soon. He felt resigned to the fact that they would be friends and nothing more.

He had spent the afternoon with Angus, clearing debris from the forest and having a fire. They then collected up some holly and mistletoe also growing in the plantation and dropped it off at the florist shop in the village. Fiona had asked if they would be able to do this as she always made wreaths and garlands from forest goodies. They dropped it off, along with some fir cones and logs so she could make a window display for her shop. As they unloaded, she asked about their Christmas plans. Angus, as always, would go away. They packed up their small cottage and went off to Tenerife for two weeks every Christmas. Mary liked the heat and on their way home they would stop in London to see her sister. Johan, on the other hand, said that he would be alone, but that is how he preferred it. Fiona had always held a torch for Johan and asked if he would like to spend the day with her. He politely declined and thanked her for the offer.

Dropping Angus and the empty cake tin back at his home, Johan went inside to say goodbye, giving them both a big hug and handing over the Christmas presents he had bought for both of them. He would miss them both so much over the next few weeks. Early tomorrow morning they would be off to the airport to fly to Tenerife.

The morning dawned dry and crisp. Johan had spent a couple of hours working on his plantation. Christmas trees had been cut down and the ground needed to be prepared so it would be ready for the next trees to be planted in the spring. He also needed to cut down any damaged trees on the plantation. With around 48,000 trees to look after, he was always busy doing something. Locking the plantation gate behind him, he jumped inside his truck and set off in the direction of Tori's cottage.

He could see her moving around inside and the twinkling of the Christmas tree lights. He pulled up on the wide drive and unloaded the wood he had stacked into the truck that morning into the small wood store she had. When he finished, he moved toward the old oak door, which was standing ajar. "Come in," she shouted from the kitchen. "I have just made some mince pies if you would like to take some home with you?" she asked, as she was already filling a plastic container with the warm pies.

Cheekily, he took one from the worktop where the remaining ones were cooling and took a bite from it. Crumbs tumbled into his open hand and one remained on his upper lip. She had to resist temptation to remove the crumb from his lip with her fingers and instead indicated to him to brush it off.

"I was meaning to ask you if you would like to come for dinner one night as a delayed thank you for everything." She turned towards him with her eyebrows raised in a questioning manner. "I will cook you meat if you say yes," she added, smiling, "even though I am a vegetarian." Again she was trying to get him to agree.

"Of course I will come, I would love to," he replied. "When did you have in mind?"

"How about tomorrow? Is that too soon for you?" she wondered.

"Tomorrow it is, about seven?" With that agreed she packed him off with his plastic container full of mince pies and his heart full of hope.

He was having feelings that he feared would get him hurt somewhere along the line. Would it be better to have her as a friend rather than nothing at all? He had never felt like this, not even with Tabatha all those years ago. He would go along tomorrow night and see what the evening had in store for them. He hoped so much that she felt the same way for him somewhere inside herself. Firstly though, he would go to Fiona's and collect some flowers, as it would only be polite for him to take something if she was to provide the food.

He dressed in his smart checked shirt and faded Levis. Checking he didn't have any holes in his socks, he put on his decent boots. He collected up the flowers that were standing on the table in the hallway and gave himself one final glance in the mirror. He could only hope she liked what she saw, he knew he would like what he was about to see at her cottage.

Opening the door, she looked an absolute vision of beauty. Her long blonde hair had been curled in an 'up do', with tendrils hanging down her neck. The dress she was wearing was blue velvet, just above the knee, with a modest neckline, not revealing too much but just enough. She had in diamond earrings and her pink fluffy slippers adorned her feet. He smiled to himself when he saw her slippers. "Come in, come in," she beamed at him. "Wow, you do scrub up well," she commented, closing the door behind him.

He filled the small hallway so they moved into the kitchen, where he handed her the flowers and bottle of wine. "These are a thank you for inviting me over," he said, and leant in to kiss her on her cheek.

Blushing, she took the flowers and wine from him and replied, "This is to say thank you for everything you have done for me over the past few weeks. Quite frankly, I would have been in a big mess without you rescuing me and Carlos, delivering my wood and then the tree and the lovely decorations you have donated, and, well, just being so kind and a friend who I can talk to." She blushed further and looked down at the flowers. "These are lovely, I love agapanthus and freesia. I will find a vase for them."

She started to look in the cupboards and eventually found a water jug that would double up as a vase. Tori had been a florist in another life. The life that had been broken and stolen from her was now bent beyond all repair, she didn't know if she would ever be able to go back there.

She carefully arranged the flowers, snipping off the bottom of each stem and placing them in the window, standing back to admire her handy work. She turned to him. "They look lovely don't they?" she asked him, turning to see he was smiling at her. "What?" she asked, holding the scissors up in her hands. "You don't need to be scared, I won't trim your hair with these you know," she laughed at him and made mock snipping gestures in the air.

"Yes, they do look nice, especially now you have arranged them so nicely." He agreed with her but secretly thought that against her beauty they paled into insignificance.

They sat down at the kitchen table and she served up the dinner onto the plates that Johan had found in the attic. She had made pork chops, roasted potatoes, parsnips, peas and carrots with homemade gravy. She had imagined a man his size would not eat tiny portions, so she loaded his plate high. "Hope that you are hungry, Johan, I have made a lot. I didn't think a man with an outdoor job would eat Ryvita," she said as she placed his plate down in front of him. Thanking her, he tucked into the delight in front of him. It was delicious and he had to refrain from shovelling it in as he would have done at home. He could hear his mother's voice telling him not to eat everything at top speed.

"Tori, this is amazing, thanks so much. It is so nice to have someone else cook for me, you know," he told her between mouthfuls.

For desert she had made a Pavlova with fresh fruit and cream. Tori handed him another mammoth sized portion. "Oh my God," Johan said, leaning back on the chair. "I think I might burst in a minute," he told her as she was packing the remaining Pavlova into another plastic container which she put by the door and told Johan to take it when he left that evening.

They sat side by side on the sofa by the roaring fire, and talked and talked. Tori found out he was fifty-two, which wasn't as old as she had originally placed him, although she didn't tell him that.

He found out she was thirty-two but that didn't matter. They drank wine and enjoyed each other's company. The evening was late when Johan got up to go home. He opened the door to a foot of snow that had fallen since he had arrived. It was even more like Christmas now. He leaned down to kiss her cheek and she turned her head towards him, ensuring the kiss meant for her cheek landed on her mouth. She had wanted it so badly but once it had happened she felt embarrassed.

He stepped back inside the hallway, closing the door behind him, and took her in his arms, kissing her with passion and warmth. She reciprocated, holding his head in her hands, feeling his stubbly cheeks and running her fingers through his hair, enjoying the feeling of being held by such a force as he was. She stood with her head against his chest, breathing in his warm, comforting smell for a short time, and then he left.

Chapter Ten

Tori lay in her bed awake for a long time that night. She had such mixed feelings in her heart. She realised now she loved Johan, she knew that and there was no fighting it. But she felt it was too soon after Nick, was she on the rebound? If she was, why were the feelings she had for the forest man so strong and intense? She felt a deep desire for him that left her feeling hot and bothered and like a hormonal teenager. She felt so safe in his arms, she didn't want to lose him. She was hot and threw the covers off. Getting up, she went into the bathroom to get a glass of water. Looking out of the window, it had started to snow again. She stood there for a few minutes, drinking the water and thinking of the forest man.

When she finally woke up it was nine a.m. Jumping out of bed and cursing to herself, she dressed and rushed off to see Carlos without stopping for breakfast. He would have a day off today due to the snow so after he had eaten his breakfast she rugged him up and let him off in the field. He bounded about in the snow with the other horses and she stood and watched him for a while. She felt envious at how simple his life was: work, play, sleep and eat. She walked back to the stable yard and grabbed a bale of hay to put out into the field. The horses wouldn't be able to eat the grass because of the snow, so putting hay out would give them something to eat whilst they stretched their legs. She sectioned each piece of hay off and threw it out so each horse would have some and would not be close enough to each other to fight. The horses trotted between each pile, trying to decide which one tasted the best before making their final decision. She stood and watched them whilst they settled to munching on their own piece.

She pushed the old heavy wheelbarrow back into the stable yard and parked it outside Carlos' stable. Taking a fork, she started on the mucking out, lifting the clean straw to the corners of the stable and putting the manure and wet straw into the wheelbarrow. She tipped the waste onto the muck heap and collected another bale of straw to put in the bed. Shaking up the new straw, she carefully mixed it in with the old clean straw so that Carlos wouldn't eat it. Sometimes he was a greedy boy. She set the banks around the edge of the stable so if Carlos lay down he wouldn't get cast against the stable wall, unable to get back up. After finishing his bed, she filled his hay net, stuffing great heaps of hay in one after another and refreshing his water bucket ready for his return in the evening. Venturing into the feed room, she measured out his feed and mixed it up and put that into this stable next to his water. Satisfied that all was done to her standard, Tori made her way back to the cottage.

The washing up from the night before was in the sink. Running piping hot water and some washing up liquid, she pulled on the rubber gloves and started on it, wiping down the old wooden table and worktops as she went. Finishing the pots, she put everything back in the cupboards. She sat down at the table and allowed herself a little daydream about Johan. She felt like a silly school girl, in love with some sixth former, but at that moment in time she really didn't care. She looked over at the flowers he had bought for her which reminded her that afternoon she was going to take herself into the village and order some flowers for her mother for Christmas. The flowers were beautiful, not something she had expected from him, but she was secretly pleased he was a thoughtful man at least.

Getting up from her daydream at the table, she emptied out the fire and Aga, using her small metal shovel. She put the ashes into a metal pail outside her door. Then she fetched in more wood from the wood store outside and set the fire and Aga up, ready for when she returned. Sitting down at last to her lunch of a cheese and pickle sandwich, Tori's feeling returned to haunt her.

She had read her email over the sandwich and her mother had mentioned Nick had been in touch again. She had said he was worried about her being all alone at Christmas. Well, he hadn't been worried the year before when he was off on a colleague's stag do which had turned out to be a weekend away with his PA, Beatrice. He hadn't worried when she had been up all night with Carlos when he had colic and she had to call out the emergency vet. For hours it had been touch and go if Carlos would even survive. Where had Nick been then? Oh yes, she remembered, he had been on a golfing weekend which hadn't been that at all. Her mother had very conveniently forgotten about all that. She felt she was being betrayed by her own family now taking sides with the man who had ruined her life.

Reading the mail had made her angry and she slammed the laptop closed. Leaving it on the kitchen table, she grabbed her keys and handbag.

She drove the old and well-loved car into the village and parked in the space outside the florist shop. Walking in, she shivered at how cold florists were. She was greeted by a woman who was probably mid-forties, with a brunette bun and a florist's apron around her stout body. "Are you looking for anything in particular?" she asked.

"Well, I want to place an order for some flowers for my mother for Christmas," Tori replied, wondering why on the earth she was even bothering with a present for her mother. "And I had some flowers given to me yesterday which came from this shop and were amazing so I would like the same bouquet delivering if that is okay." Opening her purse, Tori retrieved her credit card adding, "The flowers were agapanthus and freesia."

The woman turned around, looked at her and smiled widely, "Were they from Johan?" she enquired.

This was such a small village it is a wonder anyone could have secrets, Tori thought to herself. "Yes, they were." she answered.

The woman wrote the details of the order down and then took the card and put through the order, plus a handmade wreath that Tori picked for the cottage door.

"Thank you for your order, have a very happy Christmas," the woman chirped at her and then turned her back to continue distributing the flowers around the shop.

Tori drove back home to the cottage with her emotions in turmoil, going from feeling empty and worried about Johan and how she felt about him, to the next minute feeling on top of the world, optimistically thinking they would be together. How had the florist known who the flowers would be for? Was she now the gossip of the village, she wondered. Back at the little cottage, Tori fixed the wreath to her door with some old bale string she had in her pocket. Tucking in the orange string so it wouldn't show, she admired her handy work then went upstairs to change back into her jodhpurs and fleece. Pulling on her old jacket, she drove back to the stables.

Someone had built a snowman on the turn into the drive to the stables, which made her smile. His nose was a rather bent pine cone and his eyes were stones. Still, he had a nice smiley mouth made of twigs and a jolly red scarf around his neck. She pulled up in the small car park and reached into the back seat for her heavy coat. Pulling it on, she made her way to Carlos' stable. Opening up the stable door, she collected his head collar and lead rope and went to the field. He was waiting for her at the gate and whinnied as she approached. She led him to the stable and he made a quick entry into his stable and straight to his feed bowl. Tori dried off his legs, picked the snow out of his hooves and rugged him up for the night. Closing the door behind her, she turned off his light and made her way back to the car. It was very cold, she could see her breath coming out of her mouth in clouds. The snow was crisp and crunching under her boots. She could see that it had started to ice over already. She drove slowly back to the cottage, not wanting to risk an accident or landing in the ditch in her car.

The following morning, she was woken by a loud knocking on her door. She ran down the stairs, trying to tie the belt on her pink dressing gown. Through the window she saw the Sainsbury delivery lorry outside her front door with baskets of shopping. She had forgotten she had the Christmas shopping turning up this morning. Quickly opening the front door, she apologised to the delivery driver who was standing outside in the snow laden down with the baskets and took the groceries into the kitchen. She checked everything off and let the driver go to his next stop. She carefully put everything away in the cupboards and stocked the fridge with the champagne and cheeses she had selected. She was starting to feel excited – it was Christmas. Munching on a gingerbread man, she went upstairs to shower and get dressed.

Chapter Eleven

All he could think about was Tori. He knew she had feelings for him, he had realised that when she had kissed him with such force and desire, but he didn't want to confuse her, push her into a hasty decision and end up losing her altogether. She consumed his thoughts day and night. The night they had kissed he had felt a deep desire inside, he had wanted to take it further and had left before anything else had developed. He sat outside the hardware store in the village, wondering what to do. Why was a grown man of fifty-two feeling like this?

He was sitting, lost in his thoughts, when his phone rang. It made him jump and he fumbled and pulled it out of his pocket. Looking at the caller ID, he could see it was Tori. "Hi, Johan," she said quietly. "You okay?" He assured her he was, even though his heart was beating hard in his chest. "I wondered if you were free, could you come over later?" He was and even if he hadn't been he would have made himself free. He wondered, was she going to tell him it was over before it had begun. Maybe that was best, he had pushed her beyond her comfort zone and now she regretted it. He was so much older than her and maybe she thought him past it. Inside though, deep inside his rational thoughts, he knew that wasn't the case. Turning the key in the ignition of the pickup truck, he drove back home and got himself showered and changed.

Arriving at the cottage, he felt nervous. He had brought a bottle of wine with him, not knowing if it was the right or wrong thing to do in the situation. Opening the door to his knock, Tori looked radiant. She was dressed in a plain white open neck cotton shirt and dark denim jeans. She was wearing the pink fluffy slippers and had her hair tied back in a ponytail. She smiled at him, wiping her hands on a tea towel and stepping back so he could pass by into the hall way. She indicated for him to go into the lounge, where she had poured two glasses of scotch on the rocks for them. Surely it couldn't be bad news?

"Let me take your jacket and then have a seat on the sofa next to me," she said to him "I have made a few nibbles – well, actually that is a big fat lie. Sainsbury has made some nibbles and I have put them on plates for us. Is that okay for you?"

He was starting to relax at the thought that this wasn't going to be bad news.

"I have to speak to you, Johan. I am sorry I have had to call you over like this," she said, with her eyes cast downwards. Johan's stomach did a huge flip, fearing the worse. "You must know by now I have very strong feelings for you. My feelings are all over the place at the moment but I am not going to mess you about," she said to him. "The thing is, I don't want to rush into anything. It has only been months since the breakup with Nick, I am still hurting very much," she said to him, looking up into his blue eyes and holding his hand in hers.

"I won't hurt you, ever," he said back to her and gently pulled her into his arms. He held her as close to him as he possibly could; she felt comforted and safe there. She wanted to stop in his arms, forever against his chest, listening to his heart beating. She breathed in deeply and relaxed. She knew he wouldn't hurt her but she had to tell him her feelings. If she had scared him off she had decided then that would be for the best. But he was still there and still holding her.

"Tori, I really do understand, you know," he told her. "I don't want to lose you and I will not push you into anything. We will take it all at your speed." He held her arms and looked into her pale face. "We do this in your time," he finished.

They sat together closely on the sofa and talked all evening about his job, her beautiful horse and running, their dreams and Christmas. Tori took Johan's glass into the kitchen to refill his scotch on the rocks. Whilst she was in there, she asked him if he would like to spend Christmas day at the cottage with her. She told him she would be on her own and would be going down to see to Carlos early on but he would be welcome for lunch and tea if he would like. He said he would love to come but only if he could bring the champagne.

Opening her fridge, she showed him all the food and champagne she had ordered from Sainsbury's. "I don't think my fridge would take any more champagne, Johan, I think the hinges on the door might break," she laughed as she pulled out a bottle to show him what she meant.

"Okay then, I will just bring myself if that will be enough?" Leaving her that night, he hoped he would never be in a situation to hurt her or for her to hurt him. He wanted them to be together for always. He unlocked his door and walked into the large house. Too large for just him on his own, he thought to himself, but he would never want to move from this house, the house he had lived in since he was five years old. He went into the kitchen and made himself a hot chocolate. Sitting at the kitchen table and drinking the hot sweet liquid, he thought about what she had been through. He would make her love and trust him. He would make her feel that she would never want to be without him by her side. With that resolution made, he went off upstairs to his bed.

He dreamed of her all night. He dreamed that they lived together and she had decided to leave him, he couldn't find her anywhere. He searched the forest, the village and the stables, Carlos had gone too. He dreamed that she went back to Nick and he never saw her again. His heart was broken, he was a shell of a man and his life would never be the same again.

He woke up with a start and sat up in bed, dripping with sweat. He felt like he had not slept all night. After he had showered, he made himself porridge for breakfast. He was tired. Why had his dreams been so bad when they had parted on such a high? He decided to put it to the back of his mind and then went off to the bank with his cheques.

His mood was not good that day, so he resigned himself to working at home in his barn and not having anything to do with customers. He cut up twice his normal quota of wood that day and decided to do one more delivery run before Christmas, the day after tomorrow. He went down and worked on the plantation for a while, fixing some fencing that had come down and generally giving it all a good tidy up. He knew, come the spring, he would have to start with the weeding and spraying the trees to protect them. It was hard looking after the plantation but also at this time of the year it was very rewarding. Back inside his big old house, he busied himself with phone calls and emails and generally tried to snap out of his dark mood, but he couldn't.

The following day was Christmas Eve. Johan always put flowers on his parent's grave for Christmas so he stopped off at Fiona's to collect an arrangement he asked her to do for him every year. Fiona came to the front of the shop when she heard the bell ring. "Well hello, big man," she greeted him, with a peck on his cheek.

"Hi, Fiona. I've come to collect the flowers for the grave," he replied, smiling at her.

"Yes, I have them here," she reached over behind the counter and pulled out a beautiful arrangement, ready for him to put onto the grave. "I met a friend of yours the other day," she hinted, "Tori, the woman you bought the flowers for?" she smiled.

"Oh yes," he responded. "She was really pleased with them and said she might pop by to order some for her mother for Christmas."

Passing over his credit card, she put it into the machine and he pressed his pin. "Does that mean then you have a woman in your life now, Johan?" Fiona was being serious, Johan knew she had feelings for him and he had told her they would only ever be friends but Fiona was finding it hard to accept the word *no*.

"Yes, Fiona, I have a woman in my life now, a woman who I hope will be in my life for a very long time. I am sorry if you are cross with me but we were only ever going to be friends. I don't know how many times I told you that," he retorted, then instantly feeling guilty for snapping at her.

"I know, Johan," she said softly. "I am glad that you have someone to make you happy, you deserve it." Now he felt even more guilty for snapping.

"I am sorry, Fiona, I really didn't mean to snap at you, I have just had a bad night's sleep, which is very unlike me." He smiled at her and, picking up the flowers and his card, he thanked Fiona and walked out of the shop. Why was life so difficult these days, he wondered as he walked up to the cemetery.

He kept his parent's grave well maintained with a clean headstone and flowers on birthdays, anniversaries and Christmas. He walked slowly up the church pathway and off to the right where his parents now lay at peace. He laid the flowers on the grave and removed the older ones left from his father's birthday a few weeks previous. He stood and thought of them for a few minutes. The parents that had taught him so much in such a short time. He had been quite young when they had passed away but he remembered them well, especially his father, and all the life skills they had taught him. He hoped they would have approved of Tori and how he was trying to win her over.

After visiting the cemetery, Johan drove to the small market town a couple of miles out of Great Diameade to buy Tori a Christmas present. She was here on a six month break so had not brought all her clothes and possessions with her. He didn't feel he had a good idea of the sort of things she liked. But, deciding to go with his own judgement, he chose her a gift he thought she would like. Driving back home, he felt pleased with his choice.

Driving the silver pickup back into the forest, he had another small job to take care of before he could properly put his feet up for Christmas. He was re-attaching the rails to the post along the footpath using the hammer and large nails to fit it all in place, when he saw, in the distance, Tori and Carlos. They were too far away to shout to. He stopped work, removed the nails from between his lips and stood and watched them, remembering the first time he had seen her. They cantered along the bridle path, Carlos' tail flying out behind him like a long streamer. They looked beautiful together. He hoped more than ever she would be his one day.

He finished up his work outside and went back inside to try and tidy his house. He wasn't a fan of cleaning but detested mess and muck so he spent the rest of the day washing his clothes, dusting the large house and ironing his clothes. He was domesticated, his mother had made sure that he knew from a very early age how to help around the house. He then took the small box out of the bag it was purchased in and wrapped Tori's present with great care. He picked out what he wanted to wear tomorrow and then considered his jobs done.

Later that evening, he went down to the village pub to meet with his other forestry colleagues and friends for a pint and good conversation. They had all heard about this new woman in his life and wanted to hear what had been happening. They found it very amusing that the man most of them had known all their lives was chasing after someone twenty years younger than himself. Most of them had never known him with another woman. He told them the bare minimum, all they needed to know and no more, and promised them all that he would introduce her to them soon but only if they all promised to be on their best behaviour when he did so.

Chapter Twelve

Tori had put the meat into the oven before attending to Carlos on Christmas morning. She had carefully wrapped it up in tin foil and hurried back to make sure that everything was cooking and would be ready for Johan's arrival. Earlier she had been out for a run, it was icy and very cold, but she felt so much better for clearing her head. She had put on her cold weather running gear and had done four miles around forest tracks. She had decided to get back into training. She would feel better mentally and physically if she had something to aim for and a desert marathon was going to be that goal she had promised herself. She had returned from the run covered in mud and forest debris and had showered and covered herself in her favourite body lotion. She dressed in jeans and a checked shirt and tied her hair back from her face.

She saw his truck pull up outside and went to the door. He smiled at her, his blue eyes blazing as he closed the truck door and stepped into the hallway of the cottage. He could smell the meat cooking. He reached down and kissed her on the mouth running his hand round the back of her neck and through her hair. He reached into his trouser pocket and handed her the small box.

"What is this?" she asked. "Come inside, then you can have my gift too so we can open them together," she added and lead him over to the drawer in the kitchen, where she handed him a somewhat larger box, neatly wrapped with a gold ribbon on the top. He opened it and it contained a set of two wine, brandy and whisky glasses, something he remembered mentioning to her that he didn't have and needed. They were beautiful cut glass and of very good quality. He admired them and told her he would always think of her when he drank. She laughed at him and playfully slapped his arm.

Tori opened her box and inside was a solitaire diamond on a gold chain. She gasped at the sight of the beautiful gem glistening in the light of the cottage kitchen, "Oh my God, this is far too much, I cannot accept such a generous gift," she said, looking at him over the box. Carefully, she removed the necklace from the box and admired it

"Yes you can and I hope you will," he replied, smiling at her. "I want you to always have this and remember me where ever you are in the world, whatever desert you are running over, airport you are waiting around in or florist shop you are working in," he finished and looked at her seriously.

He made something stir in her stomach when he looked at her like that and she didn't know what to say to him. She handed him the necklace and turned around so he could fasten it around her neck. She lifted her ponytail out of his way, revealing her beautiful slender neck. He wanted to kiss it but resisted temptation. Tori had never been given such a meaningful gift and it had made her feel very special and treasured. As she stirred the gravy, she touched the diamond and dared to hope that this man would not hurt her.

Christmas lunch was a big success. The piles of food Tori had prepared were ready on time. Tori had been a very good cook when she had been with Nick and had always hosted dinner parties and lunches for his friends and colleagues. She had not enjoyed it but had done it to support Nick in his career. Something he had never thanked her for, it had just been another thing he had expected from her.

Johan had been very grateful for the fabulous meal put in front of him. For many years he had eaten alone or sometimes at Angus and Mary's on the odd year they had not gone to Tenerife. Tori was an amazing cook, much better than his standards. He hoped that she would cook for him many more times before she had to go home – something he didn't want to think about. It had been a fabulous meal with all the trimmings and a fabulous Christmas pudding with brandy sauce garnished with holly. She told him she had picked it from the forest.

After lunch, they went for a long walk in the forest. They dressed in scarves and gloves and heavy coats. It was cold, the crisp white snow crunched under foot as they walked together arm in arm. She told him of her great desire to carry on with her ultra-marathons, he told her of his dream to go back to Norway and see where he had been born and his parents had come from. She asked about his parents and he found himself telling her all about them. His father Hans had been a huge, strapping man with a gentle heart. He had showed him the ways of the forest and been a brilliant father. His mother Ingrid had been a dear mother to him but had died when he was only ten years old. Of course he remembered her, but Mary had taken on part of the mother role after Ingrid had passed away. He told her of the closeness of his relationship with Mary and Angus and told her all about them. Tori had not met either of them in her time at the cottage but hoped to meet them before she went back home to Leicestershire. Later, they drove over to see Carlos, Johan helped her with the stable jobs and then made their way back to the cottage.

Back inside the old but quaint cottage, she lay in his arms with her head against his chest. Together they watched Christmas films on the television. In the evening, they drank wine and ate lunch time leftovers on chunky bread, sat in front of the roaring fire. Immensely happy, they both fell asleep, wrapped up in each other on the sofa. Johan woke at three a.m. and let himself out, after covering Tori with a throw from the chair. He felt very happy with his life now Tori Brown was in it.

Tori woke up at seven thirty, alarmed she was on the sofa. Then she remembered they had spent the evening laying together wrapped in each other's limbs. She got up and looked out of the window, Johan had gone home. He had covered her with a throw before he had gone. She felt sad he was not here with her still. Why were her feelings running away with her, why did she want him to stop here with her? She felt safe with him, he was kind and warm and he listened to her. He was a good man and had honoured her decision that she didn't want to rush into anything. Inside though she had wanted him to make love to her from the minute she had first seen him. She felt herself flush at the thought.

Upstairs, she undressed to change into her running clothes. Standing in the bathroom, she felt at her neck. The necklace was still there, the pendant shining back at her from the bathroom mirror. She stood for a minute, moving the diamond around in the light of the bathroom and watching it sparkle between her fingers. He was so generous. She had felt overwhelmed when he had presented her with the gift, along with the statement he had made to her. She would always wear it. She would always remember him like he had said, wherever she was, whatever desert she was running over or florist shop she was working in. She thought about going back to the florist shop she worked in back home wearing the diamond. How would she feel, working there with him still here, wearing that reminder of a Christmas spent with him, she wondered?

She ran to the stables that morning. It wasn't far from the cottage and the road on Boxing Day was quiet. She arrived at the stables to find Carlos was having a tantrum in his stable. She changed into her wellingtons and quickly grabbed the Barbour jacket she kept there and went to fetch his feed. As he ate, she changed over his rugs, removing is night rug and replacing it with his outdoor one, ready for the field. James came and leant over the door to chat with her whilst she worked. He was interested in what sort of Christmas she had enjoyed. He knew about Johan, as, it seemed, the whole yard did! She didn't care anymore who knew. She relayed what a brilliant day she had with him and showed him the necklace. James wowed at it, "You must have made him a nice dinner to receive that for a present," he smiled at her and winked. She told him the present was given to her before the lunch had even been served. James laughed and went off to finish his stable yard duties.

Running back to the cottage, the cold air was burning Tori's throat. She coughed a little to clear her airways and carried on. Nearing the cottage, she walked the last bit of the journey to cool down. Back at the cottage, she could see a car parked outside next to hers. She stopped and felt disappointment sweep over her like a blanket. It was Nick's red Porsche. How had he found her? She felt her stomach and heart drop at the prospect of seeing him again. Why had he turned up now, why wouldn't he leave her alone to get on with her life. Surely she had made it obvious they were not going to reconcile their relationship now or ever. Feeling a black mood start to brew inside her, she walked swiftly on towards the old oak door.

As she passed his car, he opened the door and jumped out after her, "Tori, wait, I have come to talk to you." He ran after her and barged into the cottage as she tried to open the door brushing past her.

She didn't even turn her head to face him. "Go away, Nick, I don't know how many times I have to tell you I don't want to see you ever again." Now she turned to face him, standing against the table in the kitchen with her hands on her hips.

"Look, I have come a long way to talk to you, I have had a miserable Christmas, it should have been our first one together married," he said quietly to her. "Won't you hear me out at least?" She couldn't believe what she was hearing, hear him out? He had been the one who pressed the destruct button on their relationship, he had thrown everything away, including her, he had taken her for granted and now she had removed those rose tinted spectacles she could see very clearly in the cold light of day who was to blame.

"I don't want to see you, speak to you or hear what you have to say, Nick," Tori replied. "It was you that ruined everything we had. Five years of my life, wasted on you," she started to cry. "Now I have a new life away from you, please just go back to Beatrice."

He became very cross at the mention of her name and grabbed at Tori's arm, squeezing her tightly, "If you hadn't been so obsessed with that horse and your desert adventures then maybe I would not have been tempted by Beatrice," he snarled back at her.

"Get off me, Nick, it doesn't matter now, it is over and I am not coming back to you," she tried to struggle free and he held her tighter. "You are hurting me, let me go!" She stopped fighting but he kept hold of her.

She could tell he was really angry now and he stunk of alcohol. "You have ruined my life, you bitch," he glared at her, holding her face with his left hand. "You get your stuff and get into your car, you are coming home with me now." He squeezed her jaw in his strong grip.

She struggled but couldn't get free from him, "No, Nick, I am not coming home with you." She fought to get free but he wasn't letting her go. She managed to free her arm and tried to push him off but he was stronger than her and grasped her arm, twisting it behind her back. She yelped, which seemed to encourage him further. He grabbed the back of her hair and banged her head down on the Aga with considerable force. She lifted her head and could see stars in front of her. Realising this was now serious, she struggled very hard to free herself from him. The more she struggled, the worse he got. He threw her across the kitchen and, losing her footing, she fell onto the flagstone floor. Before she could get up he was in front of her, kicking her in the stomach and ribs. She gasped for breath as he winded her and tried to grasp his foot to stop him but he just redirected it into her face. She lay on the floor in the foetal position trying to get her breath. He went over to the other side of the kitchen and grabbed her handbag and coat. At this point, Tori managed to pull herself up onto her feet and run to the door.

Outside, Johan pulled in behind the old Volkswagen. It seemed that Tori had company. Somebody who drove a red Porsche. He wondered who it could be, she had never mentioned she was having guests or anyone with such a beautiful car. As he got out of the silver pickup, the cottage door suddenly opened and Tori stumbled out, falling onto the hard ice outside. She had landed on her hands and knees and as she looked up at him he could see her lip was bleeding and her eye was very badly bloodshot. She tried to get up from her position on the ground but skidded on ice and fell back to the hard floor beneath her. Behind her, a man shouted to her, telling her to get in the car. She stood up and fell over again.

The man appeared in the doorway and stared at Johan. "And what do you want?" he asked as he threw Tori's handbag and coat at her, the contents of the handbag spilling all over the floor in front of her

"No," Johan boomed at him. "What do you want?" He walked quickly with meaning towards Nick, curling his massive hands into fists as he walked. He could feel fury burning up from his stomach and into his chest like hot lava. Tori sat on the floor with her back against the cottage wall, looking like she was about to pass out. Her eyes were closed, she had blood running off her chin and she was shivering uncontrollably. The contents of her bag were on the floor all around her.

Nick realised this enormous man was going to cause him some real damage and retreated inside the cottage, trying to close the door, but Johan was faster and much stronger. He pushed the door so hard it hit Nick full in the face breaking his nose and splitting his top lip at the same time as knocking him over backwards. Struggling to get up from his position on the flagstone floor and away from this huge giant of a man, Nick was far too slow. Johan leaned down and grasped him by his jacket collar, picking him up off the floor and dragging him to his car, throwing him across the bonnet and onto the hard ground on the other side of the car. Nick scrambled to his feet and started to protest as Johan walked around the Porsche, ready to make him pay for what he had done to Tori, today and in the past months. The veins on his arms and on his forehead were standing up and Nick could see he was not going to get away from the situation he had made very easily. Nick was in a blind panic and managed to get up and was inside his car and away down the drive faster than the Porsche had ever been driven before.

Chapter Thirteen

Johan collected an unconscious Tori up from the cold ice in his arms and carried her inside, carefully putting her down on the sofa. He covered her with a throw. She was in and out of consciousness and shaking uncontrollably. Her lip was very badly split and was swollen and bleeding. The red bloodshot was hiding a huge bruise around her eye. He fetched ice and wrapped it in tea towels before placing one pack on her eye and one on her lip. She lay on the sofa with her head on his lap and he stroked her long blonde hair. Johan collected the contents of her bag that were all over the driveway and her jacket, then locked the door behind him.

He wondered whatever had possessed this man to behave in such a way. Although he had never met Nick and she didn't really speak about him, he had known the minute he saw him who he was. She had nearly married him, this dreadful brutal man who had come and tried to beat her half to death. He wondered what would have happened to her if he hadn't arrived when he did. Would he have taken her away? What if he came back and took her, or worse? Johan realised he could quite easily have beaten Nick half to death, being twice the size, but Johan did not often lose his temper. He had come very close that day.

Four hours passed and Tori had come round she was sipping hot tea on the sofa as best as she could with a cut lip. Her knees were up under her chin and she was wrapped in a blanket. Johan had stoked the fire to stop her shivering but realised she was in shock. She had relayed events before Johan had arrived. Nick had been very drunk, she could smell alcohol on him and he had found where she was by deception. He had broken into Tim's house and ransacked the place on Christmas Eve. Tim had not even mentioned it to her when they had spoken on Christmas morning, probably not wanting to worry her. He had driven down to persuade her to move back with him and then turned nasty when she had refused. He had never shown any signs of violence in the five years she had been with him. Maybe he was having a breakdown and that was the reason she would not take it any further and didn't want to call the police. It had not occurred to her that he might come back.

Johan called James at the stables and asked him to take care of Carlos that evening and the following morning. Tori was refusing to go to the hospital and Johan was not leaving her alone. He made her soup and ran her a hot bath with some of her favourite bubble bath to try and make her feel better. She had been very badly shocked by what had happened. That was not the Nick she had known, what had happened to him?

Tori had been very quiet all night and had fallen asleep on the sofa again. This time Johan carried her upstairs to her bed and pulled the duvet up over her. He fetched her a glass of water from the bathroom and placed her painkillers next to the glass. He did not know what would happen now. This had probably made her decide that she didn't want to be in any relationship with any man if they could turn into a maniac at a minute's notice. He was worried that she would think he was a violent man because he had sent Nick on his way. He was so much bigger than Nick that perhaps she would think he was a threat to her. He had decided to stop over at the cottage in case Nick returned so he slept on the sofa that night and kept one ear open for strange noises.

The following morning, Tori looked much worse. She had a huge black eye and her lip was very swollen. Her tooth had become loose and she ached all over. Still, she dragged herself out of bed and got dressed. She managed to walk downstairs, despite the vast bruise on her leg from falling onto the doorstep. She ached everywhere, her ribs and stomach were torturous. Shuffling into the kitchen, she turned on the kettle and put more wood in the Aga. Turning around, she screamed when she saw Johan in the doorway. Bursting into tears, she said she thought Nick had come back. He held her close to him and tried to calm her fragile nerves.

He explained that he had stayed in case Nick did come back and hoped she didn't mind. The cold reality dawned on her that if Nick had come back he could have killed her. She thanked him for his thoughtfulness. Wiping her tears away, he kissed her on her forehead.

He sat her down on one of the chairs at the kitchen table and told her today was no day for porridge and he would make her a full vegetarian cooked breakfast, which he too would have to partake in, as there was no bacon. She smiled at this comment and drank the tea he put in front of her. She only ate part of the breakfast, she had terrible pain in her stomach and ribs where she had been kicked. She could not comprehend what had happened to Nick in the months she had been away. He had seemed like a completely different person. She had never been afraid of him previously and had thought he was just going to be a nuisance. How wrong could she have been?

Her phone rang and she could see it was Tim calling. She answered his call and started to shake. "Tori," he sounded serious, "I have something that you need to hear, are you sitting down?" he asked. She assured him she was and he continued, "There has been an accident," he said and then added, "Yesterday afternoon, Boxing day. Nick has been killed." She felt numb and dropped the phone onto the table, staring ahead into nothing.

Johan picked up the phone from the table and introduced himself as her friend. Tim continued, "Nick has been killed in an accident, apparently he was very drunk, about five times over the limit, and they found a bottle of brandy on the passenger seat. He was speeding. We are not sure where he had been but he was on his way back home when he hit a truck at 120mph. He was killed instantly, he didn't have his seatbelt on and was thrown through the windscreen." Inside, Johan felt relief that Tori would not be at the mercy of this man again. Johan relayed the events of the day before to Tim who was horrified at what had happened and wanted to come down straight away to see her. "Please let me talk with her," Tim pleaded. Johan handed the phone back to Tori.

Tim was not coming to visit, Tori had made sure of that. She knew how busy he was, had kept her location secret as long as possible and tried his best. It had not been his fault Nick had turned to drugs as well as drink and broken into his house. Tori felt safe now Johan was with her and she had told this to Tim. Johan had promised Tim an update on her progress in the next couple of days. Tori went back to bed after her conversation with Tim. She felt sure her ribs had been badly cracked if not broken. She had never hurt so much in her entire life.

Nick was dead. The man who she had loved more than life itself up until earlier that year, the man she should have been with this Christmas and who would have been the father to her children that would now never be. She didn't know how she felt about what had happened over the last twenty-four hours. She was physically and emotionally a wreck. She had never relied on other people in her life, always been able to look after herself in every aspect. Now she felt fragile, vulnerable and weak and hated herself for it.

She fell into a dreamless sleep and didn't wake until that evening. Making her way downstairs in her pyjamas she saw Johan outside filling up the wood baskets. As he carried them full to overflowing inside without any physical effort he smiled at her "How are you feeling now, sleeping beauty?" he asked. She told him she was worried about Carlos, it was late but he assured her he had called the stables and asked James to look after him for another couple of days. He promised if she felt better tomorrow he would take her to see him.

She sat on the sofa and he piled fresh wood onto the fire then fetched her more tea and painkillers. "Tori," he tenderly took her hands in his, "Your mother called you earlier today about Nick." He didn't really know how to put the words, so he tried, "She wants to know if you want to see him at the funeral directors before the funeral." He stroked the back of her hands with his thumbs and added, "She wants to know if you are planning to go back home now and attend the funeral."

He looked at her bruised and swollen face as she turned to him. "No, I don't want to see him, I don't want to go to the funeral and I am not going back home, ever," she softly replied, reaching for the bottle of painkillers.

Johan asked, "Do you want me to go home now? I can come back tomorrow or I can stay with you?" He added, "I do really need to go and get some fresh clothes anyway and I need a shower, I stink," he smiled at her, his blue eyes intense. She told him that she would be fine if he wanted to go back home. Secretly she didn't want him to go but she was not the clingy type.

He closed the door behind him and stood on the doorstep, taking a big lungful of the cold night air for a minute, until he found his keys to the pickup. He started the engine. He had agreed to leave her to have a shower and collect more clothes from his house and would return within an hour at the most. She was happy with that and had decided to have a long hot bath and put more cream on her bruised and torn lip, hoping she wouldn't look quite as bad when he returned. Her feelings for him had deepened to a new level. Now she felt she couldn't live without him by her side. He had saved her from quite probable death, at least broken bones and hospital admission.

She sat in the bath with her knees up under her chin, hugging them to her battered body. She thought of Johan and how much she wanted him to make love to her. She wanted reassurance from him that she was still desirable and that he loved her despite what had happened. She felt ugly and scarred and weak. She wanted the next few weeks to be over, but most of all she wanted Johan by her side to face the storm and dark times that were ahead of her.

She thought of her mother and knew Tim had told her what had happened when he had turned up at the cottage, she didn't know if he had told her the full story but she knew that Nick had beaten her. She didn't want to go to the funeral and she never wanted to return back home. What had her mother made of Johan, she wondered, but she didn't care either. She knew he had introduced himself as a friend when she had called earlier and Tori had been asleep. He had done the same thing to Tim but she knew her mother would pry. She would try to avoid all contact for the next few weeks until the funeral was over and the dust had settled.

Getting out of the bath and drying herself as carefully as she could, she put on fresh pyjamas, shovelling the others into the washing basket. She reached inside the small cupboard and pulled out a new bath robe. She put some cream onto her lip and looked at the huge black and blue bruise that was emerging on either side of her rib cage.

She had not told Johan how badly Nick had beaten and kicked her. He knew she was in pain and that was all he needed to know. Fastening the belt, she made her way downstairs to make fresh tea for when Johan returned.

Chapter Fourteen

The lights from his pickup flashed across the window as he pulled in behind her Volkswagen. Stepping out of the truck, Johan grabbed the bag of spare clothes and toiletries he had brought with him, along with his phone.

Letting himself into the cottage, he called out so she would not be startled when she saw him. She was in the kitchen, sitting at the large table, staring at nothing and picking at her fingernails. Her wet hair hung around her shoulders. He bent over and kissed the top of her head. Today he noticed she looked so much older than her thirty-two years. He went to the fridge and poured her a glass of wine, not ideal under the circumstances, but he realised she needed it.

He asked her if she wanted food but she didn't. She didn't want to speak and he was worried she was withdrawing into herself. He thought he should have taken her to the hospital after her beating but she was so distressed he didn't want to make things worse. She had a bottle of 600mg Ibuprofen left over from her desert racing in her bathroom cupboard and he had gotten that, along with some Paracetamol and she had taken them.

He slept in the spare bed that night. He had so desperately wanted to sleep with her, to hold her safe against him all night, to protect her, and he felt terribly guilty that he wanted to make love to her so desperately too. How could he think of things like that when she was in such a terrible state?

She woke a lot in the night. She was in desperate pain and couldn't lie comfortably in her bed. It was four thirty a.m. when she went into his room, pulled over the duvet and got into the bed beside him. He was sleeping, but he put both arms around her without waking. She lay close to him, feeling his breathing and cherishing the warmth from his naked chest. She wanted to stay there forever. She fell asleep and didn't wake until the following morning.

It was seven a.m. when he woke up, realising she was next to him. He was holding her very close. She must have gotten in bed with him in the night, maybe she had been frightened. The smell of her was fabulous. He lay with her there for an age with her in his arms and pressed closely against his body. Later, he got out of bed and put on his robe pulling it on over his half-naked body. She stirred but didn't awaken. Leaving her where she lay, he went downstairs to stoke the Aga so the house would be warm for her. Putting on toast and making tea, he set up a tray to take upstairs. He placed the bottles of painkillers onto the tray. He put the empty bottles of wine into the recycling bins.

Sitting down whilst he waited for the kettle to boil, he wondered what would happen now. How would this affect their new relationship together? Soon he would have to return to work. Tori would be on her own with her thoughts and memories, would she decide to go back home now that Nick was not around to bother her? He wondered if she would change her mind at the last minute and go to the funeral, he didn't know if he should mention it or not to her. He wished more than ever that Angus was here, he needed some fatherly advice.

He took the tray upstairs and left it on her bedside whilst he showered and dressed. She was still asleep when he returned so he went back downstairs and busied himself with phone calls to people expecting wood deliveries. An hour later, he went back upstairs and woke her for her medication. She was so tired but looked slightly better, he thought as he handed out her medication. She ate the breakfast and drank the tea he had made for her. She said she was getting up so he left her to get herself ready.

Sitting in the pickup, she was trying not to wince every time they hit a bump in the road. She wanted to see Carlos and make sure he wasn't getting himself into any mischief. Pulling into the yard, James was leading Carlos out into the field.

Seeing Tori, he was visibly very shocked, "Oh my God, what has happened to you, Tori?" he asked, looking at Johan and then back at her.

"I had an eventful Boxing Day," she replied and tried to laugh. She didn't want everyone in the village knowing what had happened.

"Are you all right, you look like death warmed up?" The concern on his face was touching. She touched his arm and assured him she was fine but how was her big boy Carlos?

"Carlos is good, he has been keeping out of mischief and playing nicely in the field with the other horses," James assured her. "The farrier is coming tomorrow so will you be down or should I see to him?" he asked.

Tori assured him that she would be down to sort him out. Johan lead Carlos to the field and let him off at the gate. He galloped off, kicking up mud and splattering them both in his wake. They laughed at the big horse as he played with the younger ones in the field. She felt at least Carlos was oblivious to the horror that was happening in her world at this time.

Tori had decided that night she would spend on her own. She didn't want to be alone but she didn't want Johan to think she was a weak and needy person. She didn't want to become reliant on this man and scare him off. He had his own house and soon he would want to go back there. He left her, promising to return in the morning to take her to the stables. He was not happy about leaving her but he respected her wishes and reversed the pickup out onto the track back to his house. She watched him go out of the small window in the kitchen. She felt her heart wrench as his truck drove out of sight. She sat in the lounge and cried big heaving sobs. What had happened to her? The life she had once hoped for had been crushed. The man she had loved had almost tried to kill her and what would have happened to her if Johan had not arrived when he did? She felt a shiver cross over her body. Now she was going to have to find strength from somewhere and pull herself together.

Tori took that opportunity of being alone to call Tim. "Tim, how are things back home?" she asked. "What is happening with Nick's family and mother?" She had to ask but she knew what the answer would be.

"Mother is expecting you to come to the funeral and play the grieving fiancé," he replied. "She has been telling everyone that you are coming back home to stay once it is all over," he said.

Looking down at her fingernails, she told him that was not the case, "I am not going to the funeral," she said. "I have not been his fiancé for months now, let Beatrice play the grieving girlfriend," she added. "What has she said about all this?"

Tim told her that Beatrice had been out of Nick's life since they had split up. He told her that Nick had turned to drugs and drink and had been in a very bad place for a long time. He had realised his mistake, all his friends had told him what an idiot he was. He had pressed the self-destruct button after hitting rock bottom. He knew Tori would not have him back after what he had done.

Tori told Tim how much Nick had beaten her, she told him of her tooth that was in danger of falling out, her lip which really should have been stitched, her black eye, badly bruised leg and cracked if not broken ribs. She cried on the phone, telling him how sad she was feeling about it all and how terrified she had been that the man she had loved would kill her. Tim was shocked beyond measure. He blamed himself for Nick finding her address.

"No, Tim, don't blame yourself for anything, it was me who asked you to keep it secret and I never should have done that. Nick knew that you would know, he knew you had brought Carlos and me down here. It is over now."

They were silent for a while and then Tim said, "And how is the old bugger?" Carlos had been found at a market and Tim had rescued him from the meat man for a pittance. He was not what he had been looking for in a horse but he knew Tori would love him so he had made him her twenty-first birthday present. They had been together ever since, that was eleven years ago now. She laughed and told him he was fine and behaving himself. She did think it comical, a horse of fifteen behaving like a two-year-old once he had the opportunity. They ended the call after she promised to ring him again soon.

The feeling inside her was horrific. She hurt so badly physically, she was mentally scarred and emotionally felt torn between what she wanted to do and what would be expected of her. Every small sound had her jumping, her nerves were in a terrible state. At that moment in time, she knew she was too fragile to go to the funeral. She would have to face the people she had run away from. The questions all over again. Tori wanted Johan to be with her but she thought she was becoming dependant on him. She was frightened of what the future held for her now.

She didn't sleep that night. She drank too much whisky and spent the whole night thinking irrational thoughts. Johan arrived the following morning and she told him she was not up to going to the stables to sort the farrier, she would call James. She felt her life was on a downward spiral and she was worried she was losing her grip with every passing hour. She knew too she would have to pull herself together quickly. This was not the person Tori Brown was, she was independent and strong; she would not melt into a wobbling heap because of the last few days.

Her mother had sent her an email to let her know the funeral would be in one week and she expected her to be there. She felt cold all over. She was not going but her mother just would not accept that fact, she would not accept that they had been over for months. Her mother could be a cruel woman when she wanted to be and she knew how to hurt Tori. This was the daughter she had expected to marry well into an influential family and give her the grandchildren she so badly craved. Now it seemed Tori was a big disappointment to her.

Chapter Fifteen

Johan decided that maybe she needed some time on her own and told her she could call him if she needed anything and he would pop over later. He went home, showered, ate breakfast and changed into his forestry clothes, deciding that he would be better off at work today. He was worried about her, she had looked a total mess that morning and had not even wanted to go and see Carlos. She needed to get sorted out and properly process what had happened her. Johan set off in his truck, with his chainsaw and tools bouncing around in the back, to seek out jobs that needed doing in the winter forest.

The morning flew by. Working on his own, Johan found an old oak that had some rot and had started to cut it down. As he worked he threw the lumps into the back of his truck to take back to the barn. It had started to snow when he finished up and the temperature had dropped again quite considerably. He fetched his gloves and heavy jacket out of the pickup. Pulling them on, he thought tomorrow he would have to make another delivery round to everybody, he already had four messages on his phone. Driving back to his home, the track ahead had started to white over in places. He unloaded what he had cut that day and loaded up the smaller bags of wood for his deliveries the next morning. He didn't know what time he would be out the next day but if he was loaded up that would be one less job. Filling his Aga with wood and closing the heavy metal door, he then went upstairs to shower and change out of his dirty work clothes and into something decent.

Tori was on his mind, always on his mind. He could not stop thinking about her. Things had been looking good for them, better than he had ever hoped and now, now he didn't know what to think. He hoped more than anything that they would be together but he had seen the sort of man she had loved in the past. Although only fleetingly he had seen the handsome features, the high cheek bones and the expensive clothes Nick had been wearing that day. His shock of well styled black hair and he had been impeccably groomed. He had seen the red Porsche with the leather interior. Johan was so different to that type of man he couldn't help but think he was a rebound. He was a man of the forest, not someone who drove a Porsche or bought designer clothes. He was driving himself crazy thinking about every problem he could put in their way.

Johan had decided to stop off and pick up a pizza from the takeaway on his way round to her cottage, he knew that was her all-time favourite food. Ringing ahead, he ordered a cheese and tomato with sweet corn and Jalapeno peppers and he ordered a large meat feast for himself.

Collecting the boxes from the counter at the pizza shop, he handed over the cash and waited for his change. The boxes were very hot and they smelled delicious. He resisted the temptation to lift the lid and steal a piece before he got to Tori's house. Returning to his pickup, he was glad he had left the engine running so the heater had made the cab warm. He jumped inside and rubbed his hands together, blowing on them to get them warm and turning the heater up further. It was snowing hard again. He wondered how many more deliveries he would have to make tomorrow.

He drove carefully through the snow to Tori's little cottage. The lights were on and there was smoke coming out of the small chimney. Through the window he could see that she had got dressed and had been out as her car had moved, leaving a patch not yet fully covered in the heavy snow. This was good news, he thought to himself as he parked the pickup. He got out, taking the hot pizza with him, and jogged the short distance to the front door.

She had seen him arrive through the window and was already at the door to greet him. "Hi," she said, standing back to let him in out of the cold winter night. "How has your day been today?" she enquired.

He handed her the boxes of pizza and removed his Barbour jacket hanging it up by the door. "Yeah, it was okay... brought you pizza, thought you could do with feeding up a bit," he smiled and leant in to kiss her cheek.

"I will go and get some plates then," she said, looking into the box. "Can't believe you remembered my all-time favourite pizza ever," she added, smiling at him and taking the hot boxes into the kitchen. She was trying really hard to be normal. She had to get on with her life now, it was entering a new chapter.

They sat at the kitchen table and ate the pizza and drank wine. She looked better in herself, he thought, but he could also tell a lot of it was for his benefit. They chatted about their days, he told her what he had been doing in the forest and she told him after some sleep she had driven over to see Carlos and spoken with James. She realised she was going to be too sore to look after Carlos properly for some time so James was going to step in and she would pop down and just check he was all right. Johan was alarmed by this decision but didn't show it. He didn't know how badly Tori had been hurt.

Tori had driven down to the stables and realised the extent of how her injuries were going to affect her everyday life for the next few weeks. She had found it agony just driving so there would be no way she would be able to drive or muck out for the near future. She had told James all he needed to know, she wasn't going to tell him the full story she didn't want to be the talk of the village. He had agreed to help her out as much as she needed, and had started to really like and admire her.

They finished the pizza and cleared the plates away. It was snowing hard outside now in big thick flakes that would soon cover everywhere in a thick white carpet. Johan thought to himself that he should leave but he had hadn't been here long and felt that she needed him to be with her. They moved into the small snug lounge and sat on the sofa. Tori had another painkiller and glass of wine. She realised that she should not mix the two but she needed the wine to numb the emotion and the painkiller for the physical pain.

It was eleven p.m. and Johan got up to leave. "Are you leaving now?" she said as she struggled to turn on the sofa to face him

"Well, it is a white over outside and I have deliveries in the morning," he replied. "Unless you want me to stay with you?"

She told him she did. He held her tenderly with his strong arms against his warm and comforting body. She breathed him in and never wanted him to let her go. Tori had never had feelings like this before and she was unsure of them. She felt overpowered by the intensity of what she was feeling and worried that she would scare Johan off. After all, he had been on his own a long time. She was also worried that she was going slightly crazy with all that had happened.

The following morning the pickup windows had to be scraped to remove all the snow that had fallen that night. It glistened in the early morning light as Johan scraped away, removing it from the windscreen. He drove carefully along the main road, pleased that he had a good heater in the truck. He had spent the night in the spare bed again and had hoped that she would come and get in like she had previously, but she didn't. He needed to speak to her but it was too soon after the accident and he felt she needed time. He would give her as much time as she needed, he wasn't going to risk losing her.

His deliveries were not enjoyable that day. He was having to crawl around so slowly in the snow, it was thick everywhere and without Angus helping him it was taking an age. He was glad when he got home that night. Boosting the heating in his house, he realised he had not really been stopping there for ages. Tori had only once been inside his house in the weeks that he had known her, which was about six now. When she was feeling better, he would have her come over and see what she thought of his house, he decided. He hoped she would like it because one day he secretly hoped she would live there with him. That was a long way off though and she had made no decision about what she wanted to do regarding moving back to Leicester. She might decide tomorrow she wanted to go back and then that would leave him here on his own with his heart in a million pieces.

He showered, scrubbing himself with a sponge and sending shower gel all over the curtain. He then ate a quick meal before boosting his heating and leaving. He didn't know if he would be back that night or not.

Chapter Sixteen

It was New Year's Eve. Johan had asked Tori if she wanted to celebrate the arrival of the New Year at the pub which she had agreed to. She felt pleased he had suggested the trip out because this indicated to her he was ready to introduce her to his friends. She was beginning to feel better in herself now. She was getting ready to face a New Year and new beginning with this lovely man.

Her eye had faded a little and she had managed to cover a lot of it with makeup. The lip was somewhat harder to cover. Dressing up in high heels and the only smart dress she had brought with her, she stepped outside and into his truck. It smelt of the forest and of him. She moved her hand onto his leg. He looked over at her and smiled putting his much larger hand on top of hers.

They arrived at the pub which was full of villagers. She recognised the shop keepers and Mr Smith from the hardware store who had sold her the lights for her tree and Fiona the florist who was there with a man on her arm who looked very young compared to her, but Tori wasn't minding at all. Johan give Fiona a peck on the cheek and she introduced him to Kurt and Johan introduced Fiona to Tori, they all shook hands. Johan went to the bar to order the drinks and Tori, Fiona and Kurt sat at a table, eating crisps and peanuts.

The evening was great fun. Tori met all of Johan's friends and customers and they all wowed at her. He had caught himself a real beauty there, they all whispered, and wanted to know where he had found her. Johan laughed and squeezed her tightly to him – as tightly as he dared without hurting her. They saw the New Year, all toasting the event by the open fire in the pub, then made their way back to Tori's little cottage in the truck. Neither of them had drunk all evening, so they poured themselves a large drink back at the cottage and sat down on the sofa to enjoy it together.

Tori was on a high, she had enjoyed herself so much that night, she felt she would fit into the village if she was to stay. She liked it here, the people were nice, the stables were fantastic and so was the riding, she relayed to Johan. He took the glass from her hand and placed it onto the coffee table. He took her hand asked her what else was good about here.

She looked up from her hand in his much bigger one and into his eyes and laughed, "You, of course, *you*, you are the best thing about here, you are the best thing in the world, Johan Andersen." She laughed again, throwing her head back so her long hair spilled down her back. "And I love you more than anything in the world," she added. Leaning in, she picked up her glass from the coffee table. He could not believe the words he had just heard from her. He couldn't believe what an amazing night they had just spent and how well she had been accepted by everyone. They all loved her, how could they not? He was on top of the world too.

He put his hand around the back of her head and kissed her fully on the lips. He ran his fingers through her long blonde hair and caressed the back of her neck. She reciprocated with such a passion and a tiny moan escaped her lips. Before either of them could stop themselves, they were undressing each other leaving their clothes where they landed.

He was amazing. Taking her on the rug by the crackling fire, he ran his warm hands all over her nakedness, arousing her to heights she didn't know existed. Then he entered her, making her gasp. He was not a small man, she took control and mounted him, riding him hard like he was a stallion. She had wanted this for what felt like her whole life. He caressed her full breasts, feeling her hard nipples between his fingers and then on his tongue. Just when he thought he was going to lose control, when she threw her head back and grasped him so hard between her legs he exploded into her.

She got up from him and reached up for the throw on the sofa, pulling it around her so she was decent. She suddenly felt a little embarrassed at her naked and bruised body in front of him. Resting on her elbow, she looked over at the man next to her and wondered why it had taken them so long. She had wanted him almost the minute she had seen him and most definitely the moment she had seen him in the barn half-naked, cutting up wood. She kissed him and held his hand against her chest.

Later, he led her up to bed and they made love all night long. It was full of lust and wild undiluted passion. It was the most amazing night either of them had ever had in their entire lives. They lost any inhibitions they had previously felt, along with any need for sleep that night. They felt free.

Waking the next day, they were both feeling exhausted but very happy. Silently she lay in his arms, staring up at the ceiling wondering what she had done to deserve such an amazing man. He lay there with her hair on his chest, slowly twisting it in his large fingers. In his mind he kept replaying the events of the night they had just shared together. He might be older but he didn't think he had disappointed her in any way. They had been a perfect match for each other.

Tori stepped out of the bed and went to shower. She told him she would make breakfast for them whilst Johan showered next. He walked into the kitchen to the smell of toast and porridge. She looked at him. Yesterday she had loved him but today it was new feelings. Her stomach lurched when she looked at his blue eyes – he could melt her with them. Sitting at the table, she placed the porridge bowls and toast rack in front of them. She put jars of jam and marmalade down next to the toast and butter.

Johan was starving and shovelled the porridge in as fast as he could. "I cannot believe how hungry I am," he said to her as he reached for the toast. "You have knackered me out, lady," he smiled at her as he made the comment. "I don't think I have ever managed an all-nighter," he said with his mouth full of toast.

"Well, I think you had better get used to it then," she replied as she ruffled his hair. "And eat another piece of toast to make sure you have got your energy back for later," she teased, leaning over and kissing his bristly cheek. She hoped that he would be back for later. Tori had not had sex for a long time and never had sex like that before. She was looking forward to another night of it.

Later he took her to see Carlos, who was bounding around in the field like a big fool. He was covered head to hoof in mud and thoroughly enjoying himself. Together they mucked out his stable and prepared his hay net, water and feed for later. All this felt so natural with Johan by her side. She felt happier than she had in a very long time. He looked over to her and caught her smiling to herself. "What?" he asked, standing with his palms upturned. "My mucking out isn't that bad, is it?" he asked, with his hands still upturned. Laughing, she moved over to him and kissed him with such passion she could feel his arousal beneath his trousers as he held her. "Wow, can't you wait till we get home?" he asked her when they finished.

"Looks like I will have to," she replied, stepping back from him. He had never felt so happy in his life.

Back at the cottage, they removed their muddy boots and drank tea. Tori opened her laptop to Skype her mother and Tim, who were spending the day together. She had put on Tim so badly when she had moved here. One day she would make it up to him. She wished them both a happy new year and asked how they had spent it. Johan sat on the other side of the table so he could hear the conversation but they could not see he was in the room. Her mother then brought up the subject of the funeral tomorrow. Tactfully, Tim closed his laptop so they were cut off.

That night they made love all night again. Never had Tori felt so much passion and desire in her life. Johan was a real man in every sense of the word, he was such a good lover, so caring and attentive, but he was a powerful force and Tori was glad she was twenty years younger than him or she feared she would never be able to keep up with him. She lay on his outstretched arm, wondering silently what the future held.

The following morning Tori had left early. Johan woke to an empty space in the bed beside him and found the note on the table in the kitchen. 'I will be back later but it might be a lot later. Don't worry, T x', it said. His stomach immediately sank, he knew where she had gone.

Chapter Seventeen

She stood in the cold of the church, shivering as the coffin was carried down the aisle by Nick's brothers and cousins. This was the aisle she should have walked down in her wedding dress, the one that hung unused in her wardrobe back home. There was a huge floral tribute on top of the coffin from his family. She had not sent flowers, it seemed false. She felt cold inside to the bone marrow. There was a cold feeling in her heart. The vicar gave the service, Tori did not cry. Her mother stood beside her on one side and Tim and his wife Elizabeth on the other. Tim squeezed her hand in support, her mother dabbed at her eyes with her embroidered handkerchief, sniffing at timely intervals. After the internment she left. Not wanting to face the questions and comments on her battered face and remarks on their relationship, she got back into her Volkswagen and drove back to Herefordshire.

He was standing in her kitchen when she arrived back at the cottage, sipping a mug of tea and munching on a piece of cake he had found in the tin. She walked in, hanging her scarf and coat on the back of the door on top of Johan's. She looked at his coat hanging there and her much smaller one on the top and started to cry. She stood behind the closed door, crying silent tears and wiping them on the back of her hand, trying not to make any noise. Johan came to her and held her. She sobbed and sobbed as she realised that the last five and a half years was a closed chapter. It was over now. She knew she was moving on and leaving those years behind her now but she felt sad about what had happened.

She had parted from Nick wanting him to be happy. What was the point of them splitting up if neither of them was to be happy? She had thought that at least if Beatrice could give him what he wanted he would be content with his life. She had put on her emotional armour and got on with life as best she could and then he had turned up a complete wreck, beaten her half to death and gotten himself killed. He had never driven without his seat belt on in all the years she had known him. She had still loved him for a very long time after the breakup of their relationship. If she had been a weaker, or perhaps stronger, woman, she would have taken him back and tried to make it work. Perhaps she would have done in time but she couldn't have gone through with the marriage finding out so close to the day. Why did she feel so very guilty about everything?

Turning away from the door but not looking up at him, she wrapped her arms around Johan and took comfort from him. He was her man mountain. She knew in her heart he was where her future lay. Drying her eyes on her sleeve, she felt very tired and she ached badly from the drive. She had been through a lot lately, more than she had faced in many years. Johan was such a good listener but she felt she was putting onto him so much, relying on him all the time, and she didn't want to be that person.

Johan had spent the day worrying himself stupid. He was sure that she would not return that night or even the next day. He thought her mother would talk her around to staying and then she probably wouldn't come back, only to fetch Carlos and her things.

He had tried to do some shopping and stock up his cupboards at home but as he trawled around Sainsbury's with his trolley, his thoughts kept returning to Tori. He felt he was being a fool in love with a woman twenty years his junior. Why would she want to stay with him long term? Perhaps her mother had told her to expect to have to look after an old man in another ten years' time, perhaps she was trying to poison her mind or maybe Tori had just decided herself that it was all too much. Had talked himself into thinking he was Tori's rebound and left Sainsbury's with only half of what he had wanted to buy.

Feeling miserable, Johan had gone back to the cottage to pick up some clothes and toiletries he had left there. He thought to stock up the Aga so the cottage would be warm enough if she came back and to prevent the pipes freezing if she didn't. He had made himself a mug of tea and was rereading the note she had left that morning when he saw the lights from her car pulling into the drive. He put the note back down on the table as his heart had taken a huge leap. She was not in a good place, he could see from her face as she walked to the door. That was understandable, though, knowing what she had been through. He held her tight against him and all was right in the world again, at least in his world.

For the third night they made love all night. That night it was a different kind of love. It was not raw physical passion, they needed each other and it was that that they expressed to each other under the floral duvet cover on Tori's double bed. They were both exhausted from their nights of love making and slept in too late the following morning.

Waking very late, Johan was trying to get himself dressed and brush his teeth at the same time, which had resulted in him getting toothpaste all over his work shirt. He cursed to himself as he stood on the leg of his jeans he was trying to push his other leg into. He finally gave up trying to get ready in a hurry and sat on the edge of the bed, tackling one thing at a time. Tori had made him breakfast – bacon sandwiches on thick bread with brown sauce – to take out so he grabbed them on his way out of the door, taking a large gulp of the tea she had made and kissing her as he went.

She had decided to take herself shopping in the small market town of Little Haversham and get more groceries and have her hair done. It had been ages since she had really bothered with herself. In her previous life she had regularly gone and got her hair and nails done. She wasn't a vain person but she liked to keep herself looking nice. She had always felt on show working in a shop and hosting so many dinners for Nick and his clients. It hadn't really done her any favours in the long run. Now she decided it was time for her to think of herself.

After spending two hours in the hair salon having it cut and blow dried, she started trudging around the shops. In the after Christmas sales she managed to pick up a few bargains. She hadn't brought many clothes with her when she had moved down, only expecting to wear casual and riding clothes. She had only brought one nice dress which was the velvet one she had worn the other night.

She was not short of money; when her father had passed away he had put money into a trust fund for her. She had been very careful and invested it once she turned twenty-one. She had been reaping the rewards since and that had been part of the reason she had been able to afford to move temporarily. She thought of her financial situation whilst she wandered aimlessly around the shops. Did she really want to go back home in a few months' time? She had already been here three months so she had less than three months' rent left on the cottage. She couldn't stay longer and keep her job at the florist shop she knew that. The only reason they had been able to let her go was that they had a work placement girl who had stepped into the gap she had left.

She took herself into a coffee shop and ordered a hot chocolate with cream. Sitting sipping the chocolate and spooning the cream from the top into her mouth, she thought hard about what to do with her life. She knew she wanted to stay here. She would have to find herself another job. Was she taking a risk? Johan was the only person she really knew in the area and she had been living in an unrealistic bubble the past few weeks but she didn't want the bubble to burst. She would have to sell the small house she had back home if she wanted to buy one here, she thought. All this was going through her head and she felt suddenly overwhelmed by it all.

Gathering up her purchases, she made her way back to the car, which was parked up in Sainsbury's car park. She put all her bags into the boot and grabbed herself a trolley to do the food shop. At least this cheered her up. She picked food she knew Johan liked and nice wines to compliment the meals she planned to make for him. She was busy reading the label on some biscuits she thought looked nice when Fiona rounded the corner with her trolley.

"Well good afternoon, Tori," she smiled at her, leaning over her trolley to place in three packs of the same biscuits. "How are you feeling now?" she enquired.

Tori told her that she was still very sore but the painkillers were doing their job and she felt a bit more active. She knew her ribs would take a few weeks to mend so had to be patient.

"How are things with Johan?" Fiona asked her. "Is he treating you well?" Tori laughed and told her that he was a real gentleman and was indeed treating her very well.

Tori liked Fiona and it seemed now that Fiona had her own man, Kurt, she liked Tori. The two women made small talk for a few minutes more and then parted with their trolleys to the check out.

It was past four p.m. when Tori got home and unpacked the shopping. Her ribs had started to really ache, carrying all the bags into the cottage. She removed the labels from the clothes she had bought and chose the red dress which was quite low and figure hugging for that evening when Johan was due to call by. She wanted to blow his mind that night when he saw her. She didn't want to lose this man at any cost she thought, as she dressed and applied a tiny amount of make-up.

Chapter Eighteen

He knocked loudly on the door of the cottage and then let himself in. She was standing at the cooker, stirring a stew and sipping a large glass of wine. He went over to her and they kissed. She had on a dress he had not seen before and she looked fantastic. Her lip was well on the way to recovery and her eye was almost back to its normal colour. The dress hugged her in all the right places and he felt proud that she had chosen him to be with that night. He held her close to him, feeling her womanly shape against his large body.

They sat at the table, eating dinner and drinking wine, when Tori asked, "Tell me, what do you want out of life, Johan? Tell me what you really want."

He looked up at her over a fork full of stew and replied, "You, Tori. I want to spend the rest of my life with you like this," he added, putting his fork down on the side of his plate. Reaching over to her and taking her hand, he looked into her eyes, "What do you want out of life, Tori Brown, now you tell me?" She told him what she had been thinking about that afternoon. Soon she would have to start making plans to go back home, she had only ten weeks left on the cottage and needed to make decisions that would affect the rest of her life.

She had a small terraced house back home and a job that she would need to return to soon, she explained to him. Then she stopped and looked straight at him. "Or, I don't have to go back at all. I could hand my notice in, sell my house and stay down here with you." Those were the words he had wanted to hear from the minute he realised he loved her beyond all limits. He stood up from his seat and went over to her. Taking her hand, he told her that was most definitely what he wanted out of life.

"Stay with me, Tori. You are the best thing that has ever happened to me, I don't want you to go back home even temporarily, stay here with me," he pleaded.

They finished their meal and cleared away the pots together. Standing at the sink washing the dishes seemed the most natural thing to both of them. They both felt that things had been said and decisions made that evening that would now take the brakes off the relationship and allow it to move forward. Johan had taken the relationship at her pace and she had made the decisions. Now the rest was in her control.

Later that evening they were sitting by the Christmas tree when Johan asked Tori if she would like to go over to his house for dinner the following evening. She said she would love to. She had only been to his house the one time and was curious to see where he had lived all these years alone. She was also excited to sample his cooking. She secretly hoped too that he would make love to her in his bed that night. She immediately felt guilty after having that thought and she could feel her face flush.

The following morning, Tori called Tim and told him that she planned to move to Herefordshire permanently. She told him about Johan and how much she loved him. Tim was worried, he thought she was rebounding but he could also hear the excitement and enthusiasm for life in her voice that he had not heard for a very long time.

"What shall I tell Mother, Tori?" Tim asked. "She keeps asking when you are coming back home," he added. "And she has been into the shop and told them to expect you back so we will have to sort something out."

Tori told him her main worry was her house and the need to sell it pretty quickly so she could buy something in the area. Tim said he would arrange for an estate agent to call around and do a valuation. Based on what they said, she would know if to sell it or rent it out. He would call her back once they had been round.

"What are you going to do about the shop, are you leaving it a bit longer before telling them?" he asked. She felt that she should tell them as soon as possible before her mother did and, they had been so good to her she felt that it was her duty to give them notice to find her replacement. All that decided in such a short time, Tori felt a little bit sad to be selling her house.

She had bought her old terraced house with some of the money her father had left her. It had been a total wreck when she had purchased it all those years ago when she was only twenty-one. Always careful with her money, she had managed to get it at a very good price. She had felt so proud once she had the keys in her hand and had worked very hard to make it nice. There had been walls moved, ceilings pulled down, plaster taken down and floors concreted over. It had taken her years before it had become her dream house. Now she was going to sell it but she knew her life was moving on now and taking a new direction with Johan at her side.

She spent the afternoon baking cakes. She had decided on a Victoria sponge to take over to Johan's later that day. She lathered a huge amount of strawberry jam onto one sponge, working the spatula backwards and forth, spreading the sweet red jam and then heaping the other one with fresh cream. She wanted him to have her cake in his tins at his home and hoped that he would like it. She thought he looked a man that would like any cakes no matter what they were but she thought he would see the significance if she gave him a Victoria sponge. Also making some gingerbread biscuits for when he would come by her cottage and knowing he liked at least two at a time, she made a dozen. Her little cottage smelled like a bakery, she thought as she piled everything she had made into tins and sealed them.

She had dressed in jeans and a checked shirt to wear that evening. She pulled her long hair back into a ponytail and secured with a hair band. Putting on a little make up, she didn't think she looked too bad, with her scarred lip still very red. Tori realised that would be with her for life now so she would have to get used to looking at it in the mirror every day. Pulling on her boots and heavy winter jacket, she went out to the car, armed with the cake and wine.

Driving carefully on the snow-covered tracks, she arrived at the beautiful wooden house. Johan had the door open so she knocked and walked in. It was a lovely house, very big compared to her cottage. He didn't look a giant in this house, it was appropriate to his proportions. He was stirring soup on his Aga with one hand and checking the oven with the other wrapped in an oven glove. She did think he looked very comical in his apron and oven gloves and put her hand over her mouth to hide her amusement. Smiling back at her, he asked, "What is so funny, lady? Never seen a man in an apron before now?" He tickled her nose with his oven glove and gave her a big but gentle hug. She laughed and rubbed her nose. Pouring them each a glass of wine from the fridge, he motioned to her to have a seat at the huge old table. It felt strange, him doing the cooking for her in his house. So much of their relationship had started and been based at her cottage. She looked around the large kitchen and he offered to give her a tour. "Come on, I will show you around," he said, taking the glove off and turning off the soup. The house was four bedroomed and had a cellar too. It was very big but very warm and homely. The décor looked very tired but hey, he was a man living on his own and wallpaper and paint didn't look like his forte, she thought to herself. The house smelled of wood smoke and she liked it here very much.

Johan had made a huge vegetarian lasagne, enough in fact to feed a small army, she commented as he showed her his creation cooking away in the Aga. Tori was very impressed. He served the meal with garlic bread and heaps of salad and she thoroughly enjoyed every mouthful. For dessert, Johan had made a strudel and custard. It was delicious, she couldn't believe a man who spent all day working out in the forest could cook as well as he did. Helping him with the washing up afterwards she felt like they really belonged together. Maybe all this was her destiny, she wondered.

Later, she told him she had spoken with Tim and put plans into motion to move down to Herefordshire permanently. Johan knew she didn't have long left on her rental for the cottage and asked what she was intending to do – extend the lease or look for a house to buy. Explaining the situation regarding her own house back home and the conversation she had had with Tim earlier that day, she told him what she had decided to do. Looking thoughtful, Johan took her hand.

"Why don't you move in here with me?" he asked her. "You wouldn't need to rent or buy anywhere you can stay here with me forever, wouldn't that be the best thing all round? This house would become our house, you have a nice yard for Carlos, good riding country and me?" he added, his smile widening further.

She sat, looking down at her hands for a few seconds, and then replied. "Johan, I would love to come and live with you. Do you really mean it and are absolutely sure? You have lived on your own a long time and I am sure you like your own space," she added.

"I want you in my own space, I don't want you to live away; why do we need to travel to see each other anyway? I have more or less lived at your cottage the last few weeks so what difference does it make?" She knew he was making sense but she didn't want him to feel that he had to offer her a place at his. She told him she would think about it and come back with an answer but only if he was absolutely sure.

Chapter Nineteen

She had slept at his that night in his big bed. He had made love to her over and over. It had been hot and passionate and she had felt giddy with the reality of it all. He had asked her to move in with him, they could do this all night every night if she agreed to live with him. She knew she would but she wanted him to think on it all first and decide if it was truly what he wanted. He had lived on his own a very long time and she didn't want him to make the decision lightly. She had loved his house and knew she would be so happy sharing it with him for the rest of their lives. So what if the décor was a bit tired? He lived there and that was all that she wanted, she wouldn't change anything. Except his horrible duvet cover; she smiled at that thought.

That morning Johan was up early. After they had eaten breakfast, he told Tori he wanted to show her something so she was to get her wellingtons out of the car and go with him. Walking hand in hand through the snow in the forest, they came to the plantation. "Look at those trees in the snow, Tori," he showed her. The Christmas trees for next year's crop were lined up in neat rows, covered in snow. It looked like their own winter wonderland.

She gasped in amazement at the small icicles hanging from their branches and the icy spikes on the leaders at the top of the trees. It looked like it should be on the front of a Christmas card, Tori thought to herself as she marvelled at the icy spectacle. Johan walked her around the twenty acre plantation, showing her all the trees that were grown in very straight lines for up to ten years before their harvest.

She laughed and asked, "And is this where my tree came from?" Looking up at him, she stood on his steel toe capped boots to reach up and kiss his stubbly cheeks.

"Well, Tori, I have been a bit deceitful," he said, looking down at her and smiling. "This is my planation and I dug your tree up at the same time as mine," he smiled. "So when you asked me if I knew where you could get your tree from I certainly did and had over 48,000 to choose from." He was smiling again and squeezing her small hand encased in a woolly mitten.

"You are such a bad boy, Johan Andersen. You have told me so much about yourself but not that you have this amazing plantation. I have actually ridden Carlos past here before now," she added, stamping her foot in the crispy snow, sending small flakes into the air. Her breath billowed out in a white cloud as she laughed at him and gathered up snow into a ball and threw it at him playfully. "What else do I not know about you, Mr Dark and Mysterious?" she asked, bending down to gather up more snow.

"Don't you dare, Tori Brown," he warned, wiggling his finger at her, but she did dare and hit him in the chest. She started to run into the plantation, laughing as she went. He followed her and pulled her down into the deep soft snow. He sat astride her as she continued to laugh at their childish antics. He held her arms over her head and leant down and kissed her warmly on her mouth. She lay in the snow, looking up into his eyes as he leaned over her. She was totally at his mercy and she wanted him to take her there and then in the snowy plantation. She wanted him so badly it hurt. He stood up and offered his hand, pulling her up out of the snow.

He finished the plantation tour and they walked back down the track between the thousands of Nordman firs to his house, their arms around each other. Back at the house, Johan found he had a heap of missed messages on his phone. He played them back to find just about everyone needed wood again but he hadn't got a great deal of chopped wood left. He would have to spend the afternoon cutting more wood, loading his truck and trailer and ringing around to arrange drops for tomorrow morning.

Tori went off to see Carlos. She had decided to have a little sit on him as her ribs had been feeling so much better lately. She would only ride him around the sand school as he would possibly be too fresh to take out on the road the first time she had sat on him in a while. James had gotten Carlos in from the field and had groomed him. He helped her tack him up and then she took him into the school before mounting from the mounting block. Taking up the reins Carlos started to try and jog. Tori sat back in the saddle and he returned to walk. They walked around for half an hour, James kept walking by to see they were okay After half an hour she dismounted, James helping her down to the ground. Dismounting from Carlos at the best of times was a long drop to the ground but with damaged ribs it was just a bit too far. She ran her stirrup irons up the leathers and loosened the girth. Taking the reins over Carlos' head, she led him back into his stable. Letting him eat his hay, she un-tacked the huge horse and put the saddle and bridle back into the tack room. She brushed him off and put his rug on ready for the evening. James brought in another net of hay and hung it up next to the one Carlos was busy eating.

"How are you feeling now after that ride?" he asked her, turning around from the net he had just hung up.

"Yeah, I don't feel too bad now at all thanks, James, and thanks for everything you have been doing for me and Carlos these past few weeks. I don't know what I would have done without you," she smiled at him. He walked her to her car and asked if she was intending to stay, he wondered as Carlos was on a six month box rent.

Tori turned as she opened her car door and replied, "I am intending to sell my house back home and relocate here as soon as I can so that will mean I would like to be on the waiting list for a permanent stable for Carlos if you will have us?" she asked. "We haven't been the easiest customers since arriving with you, have we?" she enquired, thinking about the time she had fallen off and James had enlisted the help of all the yard staff at the time to come and find her and Carlos, knowing she was not in a familiar area.

"Well the reason I asked is that we have a permanent position available as one of the horse's owners has moved so he will be moving shortly. Rather than be on the waiting list, you can have that stable if you would like it?" he said, smiling at the look of joy that was spreading on her face.

"Yes, yes, yes! I would love to take that stable," she said enthusiastically.

"Just let me know when you want me to move everything around and I will get it sorted out," she replied.

"I think Johan will have to come and help me though," she thought on about the amount of work moving a stable would take and the fact she was still not recovered

"If you can let me know two days in advance I will get it sorted out," she assured James before leaving. Things were turning out well for her, she felt so happy as she drove back to her cottage she felt she would overflow with joy.

Johan called her to say that he would be late going over due to how much wood he still needed to load. "Would you like me to come and cook dinner at yours tonight then to save you having to get changed and come to mine? We can have a practice living together night?" she asked him.

"Tori, that would be great, if you don't mind?" He said that he had wine in the fridge and food, so to drop by when she was ready, he would probably be in the barn. She remembered the first time she had seen him in the barn. Standing behind a huge log with his hands wrapped around the log splitter, the veins on his arms had been standing proud, he had been sweating and it had run down his body to the waistband on his jeans. She smiled to herself as she remembered how embarrassed she had been but completely unable to take her eyes off him. She couldn't believe that man had felt the same way about her. She felt she had to pinch herself to make sure that all these good things really were real and happening to her. She was so happy she felt she would burst.

Driving round to Johan's, she popped her head around the barn to let him know she had arrived. It was somewhat colder today than it had been the first time she had seen him in the barn and he had a shirt on. Feeling just a little bit disappointed, she went over and kissed him. Running her hand over his brushed cotton shirt and around to his back, she gave him a big hug and went indoors.

An hour later, they were sitting down to dinner. Tori told him of her short ride on Carlos and her excitement at being offered a permanent stable on the yard. That was one less thing she had to worry about moving down, Carlos had a home at the stables now. She had offered to help James out too with some jobs around the yard if he needed her to. He had realised when he saw how she managed the huge horse she was a good horse woman. Her friendship with James was becoming a good one.

Johan was tired. He still had more wood to load into the trailer in the morning and go out on his deliveries alone. He hoped that Angus would return soon but he had heard that Mary had wanted to stay at her sisters for longer and not return until the snow had gone. She didn't like the cold winter months but without Angus, Johan was struggling with the work load he had on. He would fall asleep so heavily at night and find it hard to get himself going the following morning. Maybe he was getting old, he thought to himself on more than one occasion.

Chapter Twenty

The snow had fallen again the following morning. Tori was helping Johan load the cut up wood into the trailer. She had told Johan she would come along with him today on the delivery and meet his customers and help him. He had slept so deeply the night before she was worried about him. They set off on the snowy track. Johan had selected four wheel drive and they trundled along until they reached the main road where he shifted the truck into two wheel drive. The road was clear but the smaller drives and routes still took some navigating. Johan was used to it, he had lived here all of his life from age five when his parents had moved over from Norway. He was a good driver and she felt safe with him at the wheel. She was not so sure she would be able to drive the truck with as much skill as he did but she would need to practice. Looking after the forest, wood supplies and the plantation was getting a too much for the forest man on his own. She would help him at least until Angus came home, she had decided.

She was a good help with the deliveries, nearly as fast as Angus. Considering she still had damaged ribs, he was silently very impressed with her. All his customers were in and came out to meet this woman who had captured the forester's heart. The deliveries took all day and they got back home completely tired out.

Loading the truck for the next day, Johan asked Tori if she had decided what she wanted to do about living arrangements. "Yes, I have decided," she answered, "I would love to come and live here with you, if you are absolutely sure you can cope with me." She smiled coyly at him and picked up the last of the wood tucking it under the trailer cover.

"Tori, woman, you know it is what I want you to do," Johan replied, walking around the side of the trailer pulling the straps tight on the cover. "I want you to live here with me forever," he added, making romantic gestures in the snow. Laughing, they walked inside, locking the door behind them.

Lying on the sofa that evening, they talked about their future plans. Tori wanted to go back to being a florist if she could but she didn't really have to find a job too soon if she sold her house. She had a lot of money in the bank that her father had put in trust for her and she had hardly touched. She had worked hard all of her life and saved her money carefully. Tim had helped her invest some in stocks and shares so she was not badly off financially at all. She could pay her way living with Johan, she told him.

Johan told her she didn't have to worry about money, he didn't want her moving in with him thinking she had to pay half of everything. He wanted her to live with him because he loved her for her and not her bank balance, he told her. All these years he had lived in the house mortgage free and he too had saved his money and been careful but he wanted them to enjoy life together too. He was getting older and he had not really been on a holiday as such. He told her he wanted them to enjoy their life together and not be like his parents, who had worked all their lives and had passed away too early to enjoy it.

Later that night Johan lay awake, wondering what he had done to deserve such a break in his life. For all the years since Tabatha had left, he had thought he would be alone. This beautiful and caring woman had come into his life and changed everything. He knew he wanted to be with her forever. He was so relieved that she had decided to stay in Herefordshire and not go back home to Leicester. He wanted to look after her, care for her and provide a home where they would both be so happy together. Hugging her closer to him, she stirred in her sleep and then settled. He ran his hand through her hair and felt disbelief that it was only a few months ago he had seen her riding in the forest.

The morning dawned clear and cold. Wrapping up in scarves, boots and gloves, they drove to the village to make the wood deliveries. Tori had talked Johan into letting her help him with the deliveries until she found a job or at least until Angus returned. She had suggested he could cut the wood and help her load it and she could take it around to the customers once she knew the routes. He tentatively agreed and said he would have to run it past Angus when he returned home but he was wondering if Angus was going to return home. It seemed nobody knew when he was planning to come back and the winter was dragging on and people needed wood for their fires and log burning stoves.

Tori spent the afternoon at home on the phone to Tim. He had managed to get her house valued and could get it on the market in the next week if she really wanted to sell it. She had made £50,000 on what she had paid for it if it sold for the asking price. Tori asked him to put it on the market if he was sure he didn't mind looking after it all on her behalf. She then called the florists she had worked at for the past six years.

She spoke to Trudy, the owner, and explained what had happened. "I had heard, Tori," Trudy said. "Your mum said you would be coming back but after hearing what has happened to you, I doubted you would," she said.

"I am so sorry, Trudy, you have been so very good to me through all this." Tori did feel very guilty about her actions. "And I do now have to do what I feel is the right thing. I have met an amazing man here and I am going to move in with him as soon as I can sort things out," she explained. "I hope that you feel you can give me a reference for future employment here?" she asked.

"Dear Tori, of course I will give you a reference. I am just so sorry that things happened as they did for you, what an absolutely horrific time you have been through." Trudy was so sympathetic. She had known Nick and had been really shocked at his actions. Thinking him and Tori made the most perfect couple, she had been a great support to Tori in the early days. Tori said she would pop into the shop to say goodbye before she completely relocated.

She then had the job of telling her mother. "Mum, I know you will not understand why I am not coming back home but I have found someone here and I want to spend the rest of my life with him." Her mother was completely unsympathetic and told her she was just on the rebound. She said she was throwing her life away on someone with no prospects and nothing to offer. She had never even met Johan so how could she possibly know what he did or didn't have to offer? That was typical of her mother.

"Well, Tori, it is your life but just make sure that you don't waste it on someone who will not make you happy in the long run. Will he give you children and the lifestyle you want?" Tori had already decided to be careful with the truth and had not told her mother Johan was twenty years older than her, which would add fuel to her mother's already well-stoked fire.

"I really don't know, Mother, but one thing I do know is that life it too short and I will not know if he is or isn't the man for me unless we give the relationship a chance." Assuring her she would be up soon to collect everything, Tori rang off.

Her mother had always made her feel so useless and such a failure. She had a way of blaming her for everything that went wrong with her life and Tori now realised that she was dragging her down. She had suffered enough lately and now she had a chance at real happiness with a man so different to Nick and anyone else she had ever known, she was not going to throw that away at any cost.

Soon, she would be a hundred and fifty miles away from her mother and her interfering ways, and not quite so easy to contact or visit. Tori smiled to herself at that thought.

All plans were going ahead now. She would keep all the furniture in her little house and sell it complete. That way it would look so much better for potential viewings. There was no need to get everything moved down here as Johan's house was already furnished. All her paintings and photos, Tim said he would pack up and bring down with him when he came to visit, which would be soon, he had promised. He really wanted to come and meet Johan so he could assess what sort of man had stolen his sister's heart. She felt the wheels were in full motion for their new life together.

Chapter Twenty-One

It was the first week in February. The snow had not melted since it had fallen at Christmas. Tori was now back to full health and spent her days between Carlos and Johan, depending on his work load. Some days they would both go and sort Carlos out and then deliver wood. Some days he cut wood and she stacked it in the truck and trailer. Every day they got along well working together.

In the very early mornings before Johan got up, she would go out for a run. She would pull on her trainers, left at the door and always covered in mud, and would run round the forest tracks and trails. She would train hard, sometimes four miles and sometimes ten miles, depending on how early she managed to get up. She would run with a head torch so she wouldn't drift off the forest tracks and get lost. She would return and shower so once he woke up she would be there to get him ready for their day. It was hard but she needed to train to keep her focus.

Angus had returned from his holiday in Tenerife and announced he was retiring completely. Mary had decided that it was too cold to stay living in Herefordshire in the winter and they had decided to divide their year between the Herefordshire summer and Tenerife winter. This had been a very big blow for Johan, as he had worked alongside and known Angus his whole working life. He had been the father figure to him when his own father had passed away and Mary had always treated him like he was her own child. He would miss them through the long winter days when they would be away but at least they would be back for the summers. They would keep in touch regularly, they had promised. Johan was also secretly worried about how he was going to manage without him. Angus was relieved that Tori was around to help Johan, he had felt guilty leaving him in the middle of the winter months when things were bleak.

Both Angus and Mary had loved Tori when they had met her. She was just what Johan needed. They had invited them around for dinner pre-warned by Johan that Tori was a vegetarian. Mary had risen to the challenge and made her first vegetarian meal, which she served to everyone at the table. Angus was not too pleased but Mary had warned him it had taken Johan a long time to find this woman and he was not to scare her off! The meal was been a great success and another friendship was forged. Mary had felt great relief that she would be leaving Johan with this woman who loved him a great deal. She could see they would be together for a very long time.

Tori's house had sold very quickly and Tim had been down to Herefordshire with her possessions. He had met Johan. They had got along famously and Tim had left reassured she was doing the right thing. Her mother refused to visit at any cost and had said she only wanted Tori to visit her alone. She would not have anything to do with someone who lived in a forest and who she blamed for Tori and Nick not getting back together.

That morning Tori had spent cleaning the house from top to bottom and cooking lots of meals for the freezer. She was only too aware of how tired they both were after their wood rounds that she wanted to be ahead of herself and get things frozen in advance. She had already been to the stables and sorted Carlos out. She had not been able to take him out for a ride for weeks due to the ice on the roads. She rode him in the sand school most days and he seemed happy with that. She had struggled to keep his fitness up but under the circumstances she couldn't do much else. Soon, she hoped, the spring would come and she could resume her riding and running again.

Every day Tori thanked her lucky stars for this man she now lived with full time. She felt so fortunate, he treated her well and they had a nice life together, although it was hard at the moment with the cold weather and she did feel worried about Johan; he looked tired out all the time now.

At night, they would sit in front of the fire and talk. Most nights they made love under Tori's floral duvet. Johan had consented to her having flowers on the bedding, that had been a big joke between them.

She had told him she had to have some sort of flowers in her life and if they weren't going to be at work they would have to be at home on her duvet cover. They had laughed and he had insisted they kept his checked one too in case the flowers became too overpowering for him. Some evenings they would go to the pub and sit with Fiona and Kurt and chat. Life was very good for them.

Johan had made a return journey to the jewellery shop in town where he had purchased Tori's Christmas present. This time he had purchased something with a lot more meaning. It had taken him two hours and three visits to the shop to decide on the ring. He had planned to surprise her on Valentine's Day but he had decided he couldn't wait another week. The box had been in his pocket for a week already.

He told her that he had booked them a table at Angelo's in the village for eight p.m. that night. She was a little surprised as they didn't usually go out but she wasn't going to complain if he wanted to treat them. Dressing in the blue velvet dress he had seen her in all those weeks ago, she brushed her hair and added a dab of perfume. Fastening the necklace he had given her for Christmas around her neck, he leant down and kissed her.

"Are we ready now then?" he asked, doing up his shoelaces.

"Yep I am ready if you are, big man," she said, pinching his bristly cheek.

She tottered to the truck in her high heels. "Tori, really, do you have to wear such appropriate footwear for snow?" he laughed at her as she tried not to slip over in her heels.

"Yes, Johan," she replied, "I cannot wear my heels to load wood and I do like them so much." She looked down at the shoes that matched the dress perfectly and pouted at him affectionately. "Unless you are going to carry me?" In one quick swoop, he picked her up and carried her across the ice to the truck.

Laughing, she playfully smacked him with her clutch bag. "Put me down, you brute, put me down." She threw her head back and laughed up at the stars, her long hair falling down over his arm. Opening the door, he put her safely inside the truck. He was such a strong man, he made her feel powerless against him.

Angelo's was candle lit inside and very cosy. They had a table in a corner, where it was very private. They handed over their coats and were seated. A waiter came over with a bottle of champagne in an ice bucket.

"Ooh, are we celebrating something, Mr Andersen?" she asked, pulling her dress underneath her.

"Thought you might like the finer things in life for once," he smiled back at her, "instead of supermarket wine and food."

She looked over at him, suddenly worried. "What do you mean, Johan? I am very happy with supermarket wine and food as long as I am with you when I am eating or drinking it," she said, frowning a little. "Have I done something to make you feel differently?" she asked him.

"Of course not, I just thought it would be nice for a change and we don't have to work tomorrow because it is Saturday," he answered.

She was thoughtful for a moment and then said, "It will be two years on Valentine's Day that Nick asked me to marry him."

He didn't know what to say, thank God he hadn't asked her yet, what worse timing could he have predicted, asking her to marry him almost two years to the day her now dead fiancé had asked her.

He swallowed and felt at the box in his pocket, deciding that the box would have to remain in his pocket for some further time. "You have not spoken about Nick for a while now, Tori, how do you feel about it all?" he started.

She hadn't mentioned him for weeks and he had thought she was starting to recover from the mental scars he had left her with. "It is over, Johan. It was over a long time ago, but he will always be a part of my life. This year is full of anniversaries and bad memories. Soon it will be the anniversary of when we should have gotten married, in March it will be when his birthday was and then it will be the anniversary of the break-up. I feel that once this year is over with I can properly start over.

It looked like the box was going to have to stay hidden for a year then. But Johan was a patient man. He had waited a very long time for Tori to come into his life and he could wait a long time for her to commit to him. He knew it was her choice to be with him and it was her choice to sell up and move to Herefordshire permanently. She was his and he would not do anything to jeopardize that.

Their evening was perfect – for her anyway. The champagne was lovely and so was the food. Three courses of the finest Italian food, she was getting fat with all this good living, she thought to herself. But she was wondering why, when she had such a physical job helping Johan and she was running more now her ribs were better. It was freezing when they left the restaurant and Johan hugged her close to him as they hurried to the truck. She got inside and he started the engine, allowing it to warm whilst he scraped the ice from the windows. Shivering inside, she watched him scraping away like the ice was nothing. He was so powerful and she loved him so much.

Chapter Twenty-Two

Saturday dawned clear. The morning sun was bright, making its way through a chink in the curtains. Johan woke up feeling the warmth on his face, he was lying on his back and she lay across his left arm, he could feel her breath on his chest. He lay there, thinking about the previous evening. Johan felt disappointed, he had really wanted to ask her to be his wife that night. He thanked his lucky stars he had not though, not knowing when Nick had proposed to her. Johan thought about Nick. Tori never spoke about him, it seemed that chapter of her life was closed, or at least he had thought that was the case until she mentioned, completely out of the blue, his proposal last night.

Getting out of bed, he picked up his trousers and removed the box, placing it in his bottom drawer under his socks. He looked over to her and could see the diamond on the necklace around her neck that he had given to her at Christmas, shining in the early morning sun. She stirred and reached out for him. Realising he wasn't next to her, she woke and sat up in bed.

"Good morning, lady," he said to her as she rubbed her eyes. "Looks like it is a nice day outside today. Shall we go and visit Carlos and then have a bit of a look around the plantation?" he suggested.

She smiled back at him and pulled the duvet open motioning for him to get back into bed beside her. He got back in and she promptly removed his shorts and he pulled off her pyjamas. Twenty minutes later they lay on their backs, catching their breath. He may be twenty years her senior but he could give her a run for her money under the duvet. She had never been with a man so fit and receptive to her needs, so caring and yet he dominated her like she was a little bird in his hands. She lay staring up at the ceiling, feeling happiness she had never felt before.

Pushing the covers back, Tori got out of bed and went into the large bathroom to shower and get dressed. Johan lay thinking about the ring in the drawer. He wanted to show his commitment to her, to make her feel settled and put down proper roots. Maybe he was showing his age and she didn't want to do that. Not yet, anyway. Sighing, he got out of bed and got into the shower. It was still hot from Tori using it, she was now downstairs making a fried breakfast for him.

Following her downstairs, he opened the curtains whilst Tori finished making his breakfast. "Here you go, big man," she said, placing the huge mountain of food down in front of him. "Fill your boots." She put the toast rack down on the table and joined him with her bowl of muesli. She could not face a fried breakfast today, it had made her feel sick making it but Johan liked his vast piles of meat.

Mopping up the scrambled egg with hash browns, he looked up and blew her a kiss. "You are a mean woman with a sausage in your hand," he commented, trying to hide a smile. "Your cooked breakfasts are the best, Tori. I cannot believe you don't want to eat it after you have made it," he said, finishing cleaning his plate with a piece of toast.

"You are very rude, Johan Andersen, and you know I will never eat meat so don't be naughty." She stood up and ruffled his hair with her hand, kissing the top of his head as she cleared his plate and her bowl from the table. "Come on then, let's go and see the second man in your life," he said, standing up with a piece of toast hanging out of his mouth. Placing the pots into the sink, she turned on the tap to put them into soak for washing later that day.

They walked out into the cold, the morning air burning their airways as they breathed it in and drove to the stables. Tori lunged Carlos for half an hour in the sand school, wrapped up in her two jackets and scarf, wearing Johan's gloves. Johan busied himself with the mucking out and setting the stable fair for Carlos' return that evening. He watched her lunge Carlos and helped set up a few jumps for her. They worked so well as a team. After they had finished at the stables, they drove home and walked to the plantation.

The Nordman firs were standing picturesque in the cold morning frost. The rows and rows of trees all uniform standing in line to be next year's crop, and the year after, and year after that. Johan had them all in a ten year cycle so from the smallest right up to seven feet tall trees.

He had them all marked with orange labels on the leaders so that they would be harvested, leaving the remaining trees enough room to grow and spread out. He had managed the plantation alone all these years. Sometimes it was very hard work, in the spring when the frost had stopped they all had to be sprayed and checked for pests and diseases that could easily wipe out his whole crop. Tori listened as he had explained it all to her.

They walked back home hand in hand. She looked over at him and thought that he could do with a good holiday. She had wished that he would slow down a bit. Being self - employed there was no need for him to be the one man forester as she called him sometimes, the forestry commission should get people in to help him and they would if he slowed down. The winter was hard in the forest, people always wanting wood, trees falling down, pathways and fencing to be maintained and he kept going on about sorting the holes in the tracks out too. They were certainly playing havoc with her battered old Volkswagen.

Back home, she picked up her phone to see there was a message left from Tim asking her to call him. She called him whilst putting the kettle on. "Hi, Tim, all okay with you?" she asked, reaching mugs out of the cupboard and placing them on the work top.

"Actually, Tori, no it isn't," he replied in a sombre tone. "Mother has had a huge stroke and is in hospital. It happened this morning and she is not in a good state at all," he relayed to her. "The doctors don't think she is going to make it."

Tori dropped the tea bags onto the floor, clutching the phone against her ear. "Oh my God," she replied, "I had better come up then now. Can I stop at yours, Tim?" she asked, gathering the tea bags with her spare hand.

"Of course, call me when you get to the hospital, she is in the Infirmary Ward 10 in a side room."

Chapter Twenty-Three

Driving her old car as fast as she dared on the icy roads, Tori thought of her mother. Their relationship had never been an easy one, she had hoped that her mother would come and meet Johan. She knew if she had met him she would like him. Johan had wanted to go with her but she had said it wouldn't be a good idea. She felt alone without him by her side but he had promised to take care of Carlos and she had promised to call him once she had seen her mother. She felt her heart racing inside her chest. In the back seat sat her small case with spare clothes and toiletries inside. Once she was on the motorway, she managed to drive at a decent speed but it still took her two hours to return to her home town.

Pulling up outside the large 1960s hospital, she called Tim. "I have just arrived and am getting my parking ticket now," she told him. "Just keep a look out for me, please, Tim. I will be there in a minute." Sticking the ticket inside the windscreen, she locked up her car. Putting her phone back inside her bag, she walked to the ward.

In a private room on Ward 10, her mother lay in bed, unconscious, on the life support machine. She looked very pale and very old against the white pillow. Tim and Liz, his wife, were sitting by her side. When they saw her, they both got up and hugged her.

"Is there any update?" Tori asked.

"No, the doctor has been around and checked her out but they are not hopeful," Tim explained to her outside the room. "I tried to ring her this morning and I got no reply so Liz called round whilst I was doing the horses and saw her through the window. She called 999 straight away and then called me. She has not regained consciousness," he explained to her.

"Oh God, if only things had been different," Tori said sadly. "If only she had forgiven me for leaving Nick," she started.

"Don't blame yourself, Tori. She believed what she wanted to, she didn't even believe he had beaten you as badly as he did, it was only when she saw you that she realised." He took her hand. "You two have never really gotten on and these things happen in families. You are happy now Tori and God alone knows you deserve it." She smiled at him and gave him a big hug.

A nurse came into the room and checked the vitals, still no change. Wandering outside, Tori briefly called Johan to let him know what was happening. "I got here about three hours ago and there is no change in her condition," she explained to him. "Not sure if we are going to be kicked out when visiting ends or not," she told him. "I will call you when I can, Johan. How did you get on with Carlos?" she asked. Carlos had not been a problem and Tori was told not to worry about him, Johan had said. She hung up, aching for him to hold her and missing him so very much.

Back inside the hospital room, Tori sat by her mother's side on a green plastic chair, her elbows on her knees and her head in her hands. The life support machine breathed for her mother and there were tubes all over the place. Tori was tired, the drive had taken it out of her and she could hardly keep her eyes open. "Come on, Tori, let's get you back home to ours." It was Liz, standing with her hand on Tori's shoulder. She must have fallen asleep. "The doctors have said that they will call us if there is any change so we may as well go home," she continued.

Standing up, Tori felt very dizzy and suddenly had to run outside to the toilet and was sick. It must be the shock of it all, she thought to herself, and the fact she hadn't eaten anything since breakfast which she had had to force down. Apologising to Tim and Liz, she made her way to her car and drove to their house.

"If you don't mind, I am going to go straight to bed now," Tori said after she had eaten some digestive biscuits and drank tea. "I am shattered, think it must have been the drive." But secretly she was worried she was coming down with something. Just lately she had been feeling dreadful but she had had such a change in her lifestyle, circumstances and the stress of the episode with Nick, she was not surprised it was catching up with her. She would get herself checked out once she got back to Herefordshire.

Climbing the grand staircase in Tim and Liz's house Tori, made her way to her room. It was huge and very grand, with an en suite bathroom. She had a huge bed with beautiful soft furnishings. Liz had good taste, she thought to herself, as she pulled the plush duvet back and saw that Liz had put in a hot water bottle for her.

Tim had been very successful at work and made a lot of money in shares. He had also been left money from their father and had invested it wisely. The house he and Liz lived in was huge and had six stables, tack room, feed room, barn for hay and straw storage, and indoor and outdoor sand school and a garage that housed their four cars. She did feel like the poor relative when she came to their house but they had never made her feel that way. She had always got on very well with Tim and Liz and it was a relief she could stop with them at that time.

She bathed and sat on the edge of her bed, thinking about her mother. She had to face facts that she was now dying. She felt void of emotions inside and at the same time felt guilty for feeling that way. She pulled the duvet back again and got back into bed. She lay awake, with thoughts and memories plaguing her for a large portion of the night. She wondered what her father would think of her and the situation she was in, both here and back with Johan. She knew her father would have liked him. With these thoughts going around in her mind, she drifted off to sleep.

The following morning Tori walked down the large staircase to the kitchen, where Liz was making them all breakfast.

"I take it there was no news in the night then, Liz?" she said, fastening her hair into a ponytail as she spoke.

"No, nobody called so I suppose no news is good news," Liz replied. "Did you sleep okay? You certainly look better this morning for a good night's rest," she said, stirring the porridge.

"Do you want some of this or something out of the fridge?" Liz pointed to the massive fridge in the corner of the kitchen. "Just help yourself, Tori, to whatever you want whilst you are with us."

Tucking into a yogurt with some granola, Tori did feel better today. She has spoken to Johan that morning. He had called her whilst she was still asleep. It was good to hear his voice and she missed him terribly. They had never spent time apart since they had been together as a couple. He was just checking in on his way to see to Carlos. She asked him to get James to lunge Carlos or he would be getting too big for his boots. She told him she didn't want to be landing on the forest floor any time soon once she got back to Herefordshire. Johan had laughed at her comment and told her he would make sure he saw James that morning.

They all mucked out and rode Tim and Liz's three horses before eating a light lunch of salad and making their way back to the hospital for visiting hours. Sitting in the small room, their mother was still breathing through the life support. A nurse entered the room and checked the machine and told them a doctor would be stopping by shortly to speak to them about her condition. They drank tea and chatted between themselves until he arrived. Asking them all to take a seat outside the room, he explained that their mother was not going to make a recovery and the damage was so bad they wanted to turn off the life support that day. It would be their decision.

Tim looked at Tori and she looked back at him and Liz. "Well, if there is absolutely no chance for her then that is what we will have to do, do you agree, Tori?" he asked her.

She did but she felt so dreadful saying yes. Liz started to cry and Tim put his arm around her and comforted her. Tori didn't cry, she just felt empty as she sat on the plastic chair, making life and death decisions that Sunday morning in February.

Chapter Twenty-Four

They stood at the graveside as her mother's coffin was slowly lowered in. Petunia Margaret Brown had only lasted a few minutes after they had turned off the life support. Liz had been devastated and Tim had spent all his time comforting her. Liz had been very close to their mother and they had gotten along very well. Tori felt very sad for her, she had never had that relationship with her own mother. Inside, it didn't seem seconds ago since she was at Nick's funeral. It was the same church and the same vicar giving the service.

The wake was held at Tim's grand house. They had gotten caterers in to look after the food and waiters were walking around topping up empty glasses. People Tori had not seen for years came and told her how sorry they were. There had been the odd tactless person who had mentioned Nick and what had happened and what a terrible shame it had been. Her mother had not bothered to tell people that Nick had beaten half of the life out of her but Tim had told them. Fortunately, nobody knew of Johan so she didn't have to face awkward questions about him.

Tori had asked Johan to stay at home. It would not be a good time for him to come up with people coming to the funeral who had known her and Nick. She wanted him to stay in Herefordshire in the nice part of her life with Carlos. Tim and Liz had been great, helping her sort her mother's house out. They had both been named executors of her will so Tori felt once she had sorted the old family home out there was not really anything left for her until Liz and Tim had executed the will as her mother had desired.

Tori had been there for almost two weeks and she wanted to get home. She wanted to be back in the arms of her man, to be held against his strong muscular body and to feel his lips on hers. She yearned for that day as the days passed by and the arrangements had been made. She had spent a lot of time helping Tim and Liz with their horses, thank goodness they had all had a distraction and could enjoy riding each day. Tori had ridden their pony, who was mostly a companion to the other two. Tomorrow she was going home.

Standing on the doorstep, Tim and Liz had their arm around each other and were waving Tori off. She had promised to text them once she had gotten back home. The snow up here had melted and it was now late February. It was still very cold though. Johan had sent her a Valentines card but told her they would celebrate when she was back home. He had not thought it appropriate to send red roses when the house was full of funeral flowers. She was so excited to be seeing him again, she felt she would burst.

Pushing the old Volkswagen, she got back to the beautiful wooden house in the forest in one and a half hours. She pulled up outside their house and next to Johan's silver pickup truck. Jumping out, she felt a sharp twinge in her side which made her bend over and wince slightly. She decided she must get checked out, she hadn't been checked out since Nick had beaten her and kicked her and she wondered if he had done some damage inside she didn't know about. Johan was standing at the door as she pulled her bag out of the back seat of the car. He came over and picked up her bag closing the car door with his foot and swooped her up into his arms. "Welcome home, lady," he said, carrying her over the doorstep and up the stairs to their bedroom.

She wrapped her arms around his neck and kissed his prickly cheek all over. "My man, I have missed you more than you will ever know," she said to him. "I never want to be without you. Life is too damn tough sometimes, Johan," she told him as he put her down on the bed, dropped her bag on the floor and started to take off her clothes.

"Well, my woman, I don't want you to leave me ever again," he told her as he pulled his shirt over his head, leaving the buttons done up. "Now let's make up for those thirteen days we have been apart right now this minute," he said and climbed astride her.

She wondered how she had ever managed to spend thirteen days without him and his fabulous loving. When she woke up it was getting dark outside. She pulled the curtains closed and then showered and got dressed in her pyjamas and pink dressing gown.

Making her way down the stairs, she found him perusing the takeaway menu. "Right, nobody is cooking tonight, we are having takeaway," he told her, slapping a choice of menus down in front of her, "Your choice." He indicated to the menus.

She looked down and picked up the pizza one. "No choice then really, is there?" she said, handing him his phone. "You know my pizza of choice, unless you have forgotten whilst I have been away?" she winked at him and opened the fridge, getting the wine out and pouring them both a glass.

They sat on the floor in the lounge, eating pizza and catching up on what each of them had missed in the each other's life. "I am so glad to be back here with you, Johan, you will never know how much I have missed you," she said to him as she stroked his cheek with her hand. "I love you so much it is crazy," she added. "This is something I have never felt before and it is blowing my mind." She pointed to her head, making an explosive gesture with her two fingers as she put more pizza into her mouth.

He laughed at her and filled her wine glass. "Well, you know I feel the same, Tori. There is something I have been meaning to ask you though, I was hoping I could wait but I can't and the fact we have just been apart for what seems like an eternity has made me more certain that I need to do this."

He reached into his trouser pocket and pulled out the box. "Tori Brown, please do me the honour of being my wife." He opened the little black box to reveal a magnificent diamond shining back at her.

She gasped, dropping the pizza on the floor and wiping her greasy hands on her dressing gown. "Oh my God, Johan," she spluttered, "Of course I will marry you." She knelt up so she could put her arms around him and kissed him as he fought for her finger to put the ring on.

It fitted perfectly and looked fantastic. "Tori, I wanted to ask you when we went out to Angelo's the other week but then you told me about Nick's proposal on Valentine's Day and I felt the time was not right. Our being apart made me realise I had to ask you."

She couldn't stop staring at the ring. It was a huge diamond set in rose gold, her favourite gold. He had only realised this when he had bought the pendant in the same gold and she had told him what a good choice he had made.

"Johan," she said. "It doesn't matter, I am with you now. When we are together nothing else matters, just us," she told him. "Nick may be less than a year ago but you are now, *we* are now, and I hope we will be together forever," she said, looking back down at the ring. "I just cannot believe you have asked me." She was beaming and her eyes were sparkling with happiness at what the future would hold for them.

Chapter Twenty-Five

A cold and windy March turned into a brighter April in the Herefordshire forest. All life was beginning to return. The snow had melted at the beginning of March and new shoots had started to appear very shortly afterwards. The daffodils had been out a few weeks and the birds were starting to nest in the hedges and trees. The snow on the Malvern Hills had melted and walkers had started to visit the area again. Johan had been busy with the first spraying of the year in his plantation and planting the young trees ready to start their life cycle.

Tori was standing at the Aga, making cakes for a fete Fiona had roped her into. "Come on, Tori," she had said to her one night in the pub, "You need to be properly integrated into the community now the snow has melted and we can all get around again." She had been very persistent. "There is an Easter fete at the church and they need cakes. Your fiancé told me you are very good at making cakes, so how about it?" she had said over a glass of rose. Tori had agreed. She did need to integrate more. She had been doing Johan's wood delivery rounds for or with him, depending on how much work he had on, and had met a lot of villagers. They all knew her as Johan's woman but none of them knew her as part of the community.

She took two lemon drizzle cakes out of the oven and moved them over to the worktop to cool. Mixing sugar and the lemon juice on the hot plate of the Aga she melted the sugar into the juice and then tipped the syrup over the two lemon drizzle cakes. "Here you go, lemon cakes, now wear your drizzle," she said to them as she poured the hot liquid over the cakes and let it soak into the sponge. She turned the oven down and put in two fruit cakes. She had spent the afternoon making chocolate crispy cakes and various other goodies for the fete.

She couldn't believe that it was almost Easter. Spring had come very late it seemed that year. She had been with Johan four months and what a life changing four months they had been. She moved the cakes and started to pack the ones she had already made into the boxes Fiona had provided. She could get Johan to take them to the church that afternoon.

Making two mugs of tea, she pulled on her wellington boots and walked over to the barn. It was just warm enough to go out without a jacket on. Over in the barn, Johan had the log splitter in action. He had worked through a huge pile of wood that morning and it was all over the floor, ready to be loaded into the pickup. People were not demanding so much wood now the weather had gotten better so she usually only took the pickup and not the trailer. She put the mugs down inside the barn and sat watching him for a minute. He was so powerful, swinging the splitter over his head and down into the wood below splitting it with one huge blow. She could see all the muscles in his trunk working as he swung. She remembered the time she had first seen him doing that same job, the day when she had been out running and had come across the house quite unexpectedly and him stripped down to his waist chopping massive pieces up. She smiled to herself at the memory and the affect it had on her.

"I was going to ask if you would mind taking the cakes down to Fiona at the church but I can see you have your hands full, big man," she said, leaning back against the work surface and cupping the mug in both hands.

He turned to her and replied, "I can drop them in for you if you want me to though?"

She looked at him, standing there amidst all the wood, and thought how tired he was looking. "No, I will go. Think they will all fit into my car so I am just waiting on a couple of fruit cakes and then I will make a move. I will call in and see to Carlos on the way back." Tori walked over and ran her hand over his bare chest and through the hairs whilst holding her mug with the other one. "I won't be too long either," she said, smiling up at him.

She carefully loaded her old car with the boxes of cakes and closed the front door behind her. Driving to the village, she suddenly remembered the doctor's appointment she had made. Cursing to herself, she looked at her watch and realised if she called there first she would be on time. Cross with herself for forgetting and looking down at her less than appropriate attire for a doctor's appointment, she pulled into the surgery car park. Rushing inside, she just made it before her name was called out.

Closing the door behind her, she took the seat the doctor indicated to her. "Now, Miss Brown, we have run the tests we took ten days ago and I have the results." Tori swallowed hard. She had not told Johan she had been to the doctor, she knew he would worry about her so she had come alone. "Okay," Tori said, "what have you found?" She was worried that the pains she had been getting were down to what Nick had subjected her to all those months ago. She had been having them on and off since almost that time.

"Well, Tori, is it okay for me to call you Tori?" the doctor asked, "You are pregnant." Tori's mouth dropped open in shock.

"What do you mean I am pregnant, I can't be, I am on the pill," she said. "There must be a mistake or the results have gotten mixed up or something," she gabbled.

"No I can assure you there is no mistake. Congratulations," the doctor said. "Now, as you are three months now, we need to book you some appointments." She turned and started typing on her computer

"Three months!" Tori said, alarmed, "I am three months pregnant?" This was getting more unreal by the minute.

"Yes my dear, don't worry we will get your appointments sorted out so you will be brought up to date with everything." She smiled at her and patted her hand.

Tori left the surgery in a bubble of unreality and outright sheer panic. She couldn't think straight. Dropping the cakes off at the church, she didn't stop to speak with Fiona or the vicar, making some excuse she had to get to Carlos, she quickly got back into her car and drove to the stables.

She stood in Carlos' stable as it all started to fit into place. Three months, when they had just started their relationship, she had been through hell and back with Nick but she had continued to take her pills not missing a day. The doctor had told her these things happen but not to her, not to Tori Brown. Now she was going to have to tell Johan, what would he say? They had never talked about having children, she had thought he was happy as they were. He was going to be fifty-three soon, did he want to be a father at that age? She put her hand on her stomach. The poor child inside, she had still been drinking, although not to excess these days as it made her feel sick after more than half a glass. She had been loading and unloading wood, riding and seeing to Carlos without a thought that she might be pregnant. A silent tear slipped down her cheek as the thoughts ran through her head.

Carlos had finished his dinner and she had rugged him up for the night. Leaving the stable yard, it was getting dark. She was filled with dread. What would she do if Johan didn't want to keep the baby or was cross with her? She didn't want to risk losing him at any cost but she had always wanted to have children. Whatever the cost, she realised that she had to tell him and face the consequences.

Pulling in next to his truck, she turned off the ignition and lights. Sitting in her little car, she gathered her thoughts and courage before going inside to him. He was in the shower so she sat on the bed and waited for him to finish. He came out with a towel wrapped around his waist, still dripping wet.

"Hey beautiful," he said to her, seeing her on the bed. "Are you up for some action?" he asked, whipping the towel away from himself and throwing it behind him onto the bathroom floor.

She smiled but inside she felt terribly sick. What if she lost him, if he told her to leave? He came over, sensing her mood and pulled on a pair of shorts.

"What's the matter, lady?" He took her hand in his, something he always did if she was concerned or worried, and looked at her with his piercing blue eyes.

"Johan, I have something to tell you. Something that will change our relationship forever. Please don't be cross with me about this," she said. "I am pregnant." There – it was out in the open now.

Staring hard at him she couldn't believe his reaction. "Pregnant? How did that happen then?" he asked, his eyebrows raised so high she thought they would vanish into his mop of grey hair.

"Well, there is only one way it can happen and we have certainly been doing enough of it over the past few months," she replied.

He laughed light heartedly and then leaped up from the bed. "Tori, that is amazing news, that is the best thing I have ever heard. Oh my God, I am going to be a DAD!" he shouted and pulled her up from the bed and hugged her so tight she could hardly breathe. "Thank you, Tori, thank you for making me the happiest man alive." Tori was so relieved she was laughing and crying at the same time.

Chapter Twenty-Six

The nurse turned to them both, smiling. "There is no mistake, you are expecting triplets," she confirmed. They looked at each other, back to the screen and then at the nurse. "Congratulations," she said.

Tori slid off the couch and pulled her top back down, tucking it firmly into her jeans. Triplets, she had only just found out she was pregnant and now she was having triplets.

"Damn good job we have got a big house," Johan said, smiling down at her as they walked out of the hospital. He held her small hand inside his huge one. "Didn't factor this one into the equation, did we?" he said, turning to her and smiling.

Tori was still trying to take it all in. She was so happy to find out she was to be having his baby now she would have two extra babies to be overjoyed with. She was worrying to herself wondering how she would look after three children. Nobody in her family had children she didn't know the first thing about looking after them. When she had been with Nick she had hoped her mother would be around to help her but now who knew what she would do? She would have to slow down a bit on the wood deliveries but now summer was coming people wouldn't want so much anyway. James would always help out with Carlos and Fiona had offered her part time work in the florist if she wanted it, to help with wedding flowers and such.

Inside the silver pickup truck, he leaned over to her and put his large hand on her stomach, "Hello, little ones, this is your dad speaking," he said. "Do you think Mum would like to go out for dinner tonight to celebrate our news?" he asked her stomach.

She pinched his ear as he was bent over her and replied, "Yes, Mummy would like to go out for dinner, she is starving, feeding all three of us all day."

Once they got home, Tori called Tim and told him the news. "Oh my God, Tori," he said to her. "I didn't even know you were planning a family, are you sure it isn't too soon?"

"Well, they were not exactly planned. I am not sure what happened as I have not missed any pills but, here we are, three months down the line and three little babies inside."

"Three babies inside, did you say three, my God Tori?" He almost dropped the phone at his end and she could hear him shouting Liz to come to the phone.

"Yes, Tim, three babies. We are having triplets in October." They were both really pleased to hear her news but down inside Tim was worried about his sister, all this was happening so quickly, she had only known Johan a few months, she had known Nick five years before she had found out what he was like.

Johan had not been able to contain himself and had called Angus and Mary, now back in the UK and back home. Angus had congratulated them both and offered babysitting services if needed. Mary had told them she was getting her knitting needles out to ensure the little ones would be warm enough if there should be another winter as bad as the last one. Angus had also offered to come out of retirement for a while over the summer to help out and relieve the burden from Tori. They were such kind people and Johan had missed them over that winter.

Angelo's was busy when they walked in and were shown a table over by the window. "Do you want to get married before the babies come?" Johan asked her as they sat, he drinking a beer and she a lemonade.

"No, Johan, there is no rush and I don't really want to walk down the aisle looking like a weeble," she told him.

"You do still want to get married, don't you?" he asked, looking worriedly at her.

"Of course I do, just not yet." She took a sip of her drink and put it back down as her starter arrived – tomato soup.

"Do you like any particular names for the babies?" she asked him. He said that he hadn't really thought that much about it he was too excited about the news that they were expecting

"Well, with three babies we are both sure to get a name we want plus one over," she said, looking down at her stomach. "I just cannot believe there are three in there," she said. "Do triplets run in your family, Johan?" she asked him, spooning in the warm soup.

"No," he replied. "My parents only had me, they couldn't have any more children," he said sadly.

"That is why I am so happy we are having all ours in one batch – unless you want more?" he said, laughing at the shocked look on her face.

Tori just could not have predicted his reaction when she had told him she was pregnant. He had been overjoyed and in the time since he had been decorating nurseries and getting her to look online at cots and buggies which he had insisted must be forest proof! He had it all planned out; they would share the baby duties, he was happy to get up in the night and do feeds, nappies and anything else so she would not be too tired with it all. He had told her that she must still keep her Carlos time and he was happy to look after the babies then too. She had said she would have them afternoon and evening so he could do deliveries and forest work and he would have them in the barn with him whilst he was cutting up wood.

She lay in bed the following morning, wondering how many mornings like that she would have once the babies came along. She was so excited. She had hoped for a family with Nick but then had resigned herself to the fact she would probably not have children at all. She felt her life could not get any better at that point. Getting up, she looked out of the curtains at what the day outside held. It was sunny and looked like a nice day for a walk around the plantation to check it out. She showered and dressed and went down to make a fry up for Johan. Twenty minutes later he was at the table, munching on his fried breakfast.

"Do you think we will have mornings like this come October?" he asked her, smiling his amazing smile and melting her heart as he did so.

"No, Johan, we will not have mornings like this for possibly another twenty years after October." she said.

"Come here, woman," he motioned for her to go over to him and he pulled up her fleece and kissed her swollen stomach three times "Morning, little ones, it's your daddy speaking. We are going for a walk around the plantation if that is okay with you all?" He took a big bite of toast and pulled her fleece back down, covering the growing bulge.

"Eat up then, big man, if we are going round the plantation. Don't have all day, you know." She kissed him on his stubbly cheek and held his head against her stomach cherishing his very being.

Johan had spent most of the last week working in the plantation. He had been mowing the grass around the young trees he had just planted in there. Tori had helped to mow, she was quite able to use the ride-on mower round the trees. Johan had been inspecting the trees for any signs of diseases or pests, something she had teased him of becoming obsessed about. He was training Tori in the art of Christmas tree farming too and she loved it.

As they walked around the plantation, he showed her where he had been planting. "This crop will be ready in about nine to ten years," he told her. "They grow about a foot a year so depending on what the trend is they may be cut earlier or go on to ten years." He was so enthusiastic about it all she thought it was funny and laughed at him.

"Johan, you will soon be able to dress up as Father Christmas when you bring our tree home," she told him. "When the bambinos have arrived." He looked down at her and squeezed her hand. "Tori, I cannot tell you how happy you have made me in the last few months," he said. "I thought I would be here on my own for ever and now, four months on, I am the happiest man in the world." He picked her up and swung her around, making her laugh as he did so.

They arrived back home to an envelope on the doormat. "Oh, it is from Tim," Tori said, as she bent down to pick it up. "It must mean that they have sorted out my mother's stuff now." She opened it and a cheque fell out onto the wooden floor. Bending over, she picked it up. Tim had put in a brief note to say that their mother's house and possessions had all now been sold and this was her share as her mother's wishes: £250,000. Tori stared at the cheque for a very long time. She had such divided feelings. She and her mother had never really gotten along, her mother had expected Tori to be someone she wasn't and didn't want to be. She didn't know how she felt inside now all this had come to an end.

Later that afternoon, she called Tim and thanked him for sorting everything out for them.

"I didn't want to tell you it was on its way when I spoke to you yesterday, Tori," Tim advised.

"You were on such a high with the baby news I didn't want to bring you crashing down to earth again," he explained. "How do you feel about it all?"

She told him she wasn't sure how she felt about it and the feelings that she had failed her mother had all come to the surface again

"You know Mother would be horrified if she saw me now," she told Tim. "She wanted me married to a rich chap with a large house and a fancy car, she didn't really seem to mind that much that he cheated on me and then tried to beat me to a pulp," Tori said, feeling she might cry and was trying to sound normal to her big brother.

"Tori, I told Mother what had happened to you and she was devastated," Tim explained. "I told her that what he had was not worth having and that you could do so much better. She wouldn't listen to me but she did listen to Liz. I know Mother was sorry for what she had put you through and what she expected from you," he told her. "So you do need to keep that money and invest it well, those three babies will cost you a lot," he joked.

Chapter Twenty-Seven

It was now July in the beautiful county of Herefordshire. Johan and Tori had just spent their first holiday together in Norway. They had visited the small village Johan had been born in on the south coast. They had a lovely time, she had enjoyed seeing his home country, he was so proud. They visited the house where he had been born and raised until he was five years old. They had wonderful weather and it was light almost all of the night. Tori felt it important that they went so he could tell their children about it once they were old enough. She knew he had wanted to go back and see his birthplace for many years, it had been one of the first things he had told her when she had been going on about her desert marathons. Yes, she thought, the desert marathons she had so badly wanted to go back to when she had been standing out in the cold winter forest that day. Now she was six months pregnant and stood no chance of doing another desert ultra-marathon. She smiled to herself, running her hand over the very large bulge that was growing under her T- shirt – the marathons could wait.

She had been down to see Carlos that afternoon and had lunged him. Watching him working on the circle around her, she pushed him into a canter. He was a large horse and took some holding onto when he wanted to go so she brought him back a walk and put up some jumps to work him a little harder. Poor Carlos was sweating by the time she had finished working him. Leading him around the sand school to cool him down, she waved to James, who had just come out to do evening stables.

James was now riding Carlos on a regular basis, Tori couldn't get up onto his back with the expanding baby bulge and she trusted James. They had become good friends in the last few months. She had been so grateful he had given her a permanent stable for Carlos and he had been grateful for the help Tori gave him when one of his staff had taken a bad fall and had been out of action for several weeks. Tori had taken up the challenge and had covered the mucking out, grooming and feeding of four other horses as well as her own. She had seen James was a very good rider and she knew Carlos would excel in his charge. Things were good now.

"Johan, come on, we are supposed to be at Angelo's for seven thirty and it is seven twenty now," she shouted up the stairs to him. They were out having a meal with Fiona and Kurt to celebrate Johan's fifty-third birthday.

Descending the stairs, he was still doing up his shirt buttons. "I am ready now," he said, kissing her on the cheek. "Come on, let's go." She drove the truck as she could hardly get in behind the wheel of her car now.

Fiona and Kurt were already at the table when they hurried in five minutes late. "Sorry both," Tori said, a little breathless. "It is taking him longer to get ready now he is a year older," she said, joking at Johan's expense.

"Yes, that and the fact that it takes Tori so long now she dresses for four people," he cheeked back at her, pulling the chair out so she could sit down.

Fiona had brought an arrangement with her and handed it over to Tori. "Here, Tori, a little something for you. I didn't properly thank you for helping me out with that wedding last minute," she smiled and thanked her for the kind gift.

"It was no problem, Fiona, I was just pleased that I could help you at short notice and it was nice to keep my hand in with the floristry. I was worried I might have forgotten," she joked.

Fiona stood up and leant over the table. "And we got you a bottle of whiskey, Johan. Think you might be needing it to sleep in a few months' time." She handed over the bottle bag and he pecked her on the cheek. They chatted into the early hours, ate great food and drank lovely wine, apart from Tori who was on lemonade. She didn't mind, it was a very small price to pay for three babies.

Johan was outside working in the forest when she awoke the next morning. He had left her a note on the kitchen table to let her know he would be back at lunch time, after he had finished the fencing job

Angus was helping him with. She sighed and put the note back down on the table. The babies were very active this morning – she could feel them moving around inside her. Sitting at the table, she drank the tea and listened to the message on her answer phone.

"Tori. I am so sorry to ask but can you help me out again today?" It was Fiona. "I am so short staffed and I have a wedding tomorrow. Can you ring me back as soon as you get this message?" Her voice was anxious. Fiona had been having a lot of problems with her assistant, who was going through a messy divorce. Tori picked up the phone and told her she would be there in an hour.

She enjoyed the day helping Fiona out with the flowers for a wedding in the church in their village. Once they had constructed the arrangements, they carried them together to the church and put them in place inside. They looked fabulous, two massive pedestal arrangements and smaller ones for the ends of the aisles. This was going to be a very grand wedding, she thought to herself as she helped Fiona fasten the flowers to the ends of the aisles. Back at Fiona's shop, she helped with the bridesmaid's bouquets and the clearing up after they had finished. Fiona was expecting the bouquets to be collected the following morning so they placed the all in water and locked up for the night.

Tori was exhausted when she got home. Johan found her asleep in the chair by the fireplace. She was stretching herself too far in too many directions, he thought as he looked down at her and covered her with a throw. She needed to take more care of herself.

She woke to the smell of Italian food cooking in the Aga. The air was heavy with a rich garlic smell wafting in from the kitchen to her. Stretching, she yawned loudly, got up and walked into the kitchen "Hello, sleeping beauty," Johan said to her as he was mixing up sauce for the vegetarian lasagne. "If you go and get a shower, dinner will be ready in about half an hour," he said, waving the wooden spoon indicating upstairs. She smiled at him. He was amazing. He had been out all day in the forest, working himself half to death and was now making dinner for her.

"Thanks, Johan, what would I do without you?" she walked over to him and kissed him on the lips.

"Well, you wouldn't be heavily pregnant without me," he told her, holding her close to him. "Now go and get a shower, put your pyjamas and that sexy fluffy pink dressing gown on and meet me in half an hour." He lovingly patted her on the bottom as she turned to go.

Chapter Twenty-Eight

Tori was finding being pregnant very difficult. She was frustrated at what she now found she was unable to do in her everyday life. She had ridden Carlos for as long as she could but was now unable to get onto him so she had decided to lunge him. She now realised that was getting too much for her after he had been very excited one day and almost pulled her off her feet so had decided to hand his exercise routine over to James. She was cross with herself. She had hoped she would be able to continue doing all she could before she was pregnant. She still helped out on the stable yard but mucking out took her twice as long as normal and she was getting moody. She was finding getting into her car a task and she always had to pee. Her body wasn't her own anymore, it was being invaded by children and irrational hormones. It was the hormones that were the worst thing, one minute she would feel all right and the next she would be in floods of tears. She didn't know why, she was with the man she loved and having his children so why was she always so irrational?

Johan looked after her very well, not allowing her to do anything that might be a danger to her or the babies. That morning she had returned from the stables feeling especially cross with life. She had been watching James school Carlos and had missed riding him so badly. She had come away from the stables and had cried in her car. She felt like her life would soon not be her own and she was starting to realise the implications having three babies would have on her. Johan walked into the kitchen and greeted her with a kiss. She didn't want him to see she had been crying and turned her face away. She had never done this before.

He took her by her shoulders and turned her to face him. "Tori, whatever is the matter," he said, full of concern. "What has happened, is Carlos okay?" he asked her, still holding her shoulders.

"Johan," she replied. "I don't know how I am going to cope with three babies. I can't do anything anymore and it is driving me crazy," she wept into his shoulder. "I am totally useless, can't help you with anything and cannot even help at the yard without everything taking me twice as long."

He took her shoulders and stepped back from her. Looking down into her red face, he replied, "Tori, these are our babies, we will look after them together, the burden will not be just with you. I am sorry you will have to carry on carrying them around for another few weeks but soon you will be able to go back to everything you did before." He held her again and she sobbed. She was feeling very emotional these days and was finding it very hard to control her moods and outbursts.

The following morning, Tori was feeling better and took herself off into town to buy baby clothes, bottles and formula. They didn't know what sex the babies would be so she just bought everything unisex. Carrying the large bags of bedding and clothing back to the car, she bumped into Mary.

"My goodness, Tori, should you be carrying those big bags in your condition?" She rushed to her rescue and helped her load them into the truck. "What have you been buying?" she asked. Tori showed her the baby clothes and bedding she had in her bags.

"Three babies, Mary. That means a lot of clothes and even more washing. Thought I would start and get us prepared," she smiled at the old lady in front of her.

"How are you both?" she enquired. Mary told her that they were looking forward to going back to Tenerife in October, she hoped that she, Johan and the babies would come over to visit at some stage before they returned to the UK next spring. Tori thought that was an ambitious idea, she couldn't even imagine doing the weekly shop with three children at that time.

Fiona had roped Tori into making cakes again for the August bank holiday fete at the church. She had also asked her to help out on the day. Tori had not been very happy about the idea, she complained that she looked like a hippo, waddling along, and she had wanted to stay at home and lock herself away. Fiona had gotten cross with her and told her she was to stop feeling sorry for herself. Tori had taken the telling off in the manner it was intended and had agreed to help. Loading all the cakes into the truck, Johan dropped her off at the church gates and said he would come and collect her later that day.

Walking up to the church on the narrow gravel path, Tori felt a sharp pain in her side. Standing back up slowly, she had another one, which was much sharper this time. She tried to stand back up and walked to the bench in the churchyard. She sat on the bench for a moment, getting her breath. She thought she had indigestion or something, as she had hurried her breakfast so she wouldn't be late. She stood up and managed to get to the church when suddenly her waters broke. Staring down at the floor beneath her feet, she felt instant panic. The babies couldn't be coming yet, they were six weeks early. The felt a huge pain surge though her body and realised that the babies were coming and she would have to get to the hospital quickly.

Fiona saw what had happened and ran to her aid. "Kurt, get the car, get the car now and call the hospital!" she shouted to Kurt, who was looking horrified at what was unfolding in front of him. He scuttled off and fetched his car, arriving at the church with a screech of rubber tyres.

Tori gasped as another wave of pain hit her. She went down onto her knees in the church and screamed, grasping her stomach. Kurt and Fiona managed to get her onto her feet and into Kurt's car. On the way to the hospital Tori was incoherent.

"Tori, where is Johan, where has he gone to work this morning?" Fiona was trying to get an answer out of her laying on the back seat "I need to call him Tori, where is he?" She was trying his phone on redial but there seemed to be no reception and his phone just kept going onto answer service. Kurt was driving the car like a formula one driver and pulled up outside the accident and emergency doors.

He jumped out of the driving seat and opened the door, helping a very helpless Tori out of the back seat.

At the hospital, she was put into a wheelchair and Fiona wheeled her to the reception. She was hurriedly explaining they had just called through and that Tori had gone into labour six weeks early with triplets. Tori was in terrible agony and was taken straight through to the maternity ward to be checked out.

"Fiona, they can't be coming yet," she said between gasps "They are six weeks early, they can't be coming."

Fiona was trying to calm Tori and get through to Johan. "Kurt, please go outside and see if you can get hold of Johan on my phone," she said, handing the mobile to him. "Keep trying, he is probably in a part of the forest with no reception," she said.

Fiona stayed with Tori and held her hand. She tried to comfort her, to tell her she was in the best place for something like this to happen, but she was terribly worried about what was going to happen to her friend and her six week premature babies. She felt guilty for making her go to the church; she should have stayed at home and rested. Fiona was panicking and worrying that Johan was not going to be able to be contacted. What if something went terribly wrong and she had to tell him?

Tori was wracked with contractions. The doctor had told her she was in labour and it was too late to do anything about it. She lay in the hospital bed with a team of people coming in and out of the room, examining her and monitoring her situation. Fiona was outside the room, sitting in the corridor listening to her screams. Kurt was still trying to get Johan on the phone. Tori had never felt such agony in her life and thought that she would die giving birth. She lay on the bed and wondered where the hell Johan was, why wasn't he here and would he even be there for the birth of their babies? She needed him, she was absolutely terrified.

Sweat was running down her red face and neck and she felt panic rising and threatening to take over inside her. What if the babies were injured, or worse? Where was Johan? Why were the babies coming early? Thoughts churned through her head. The contractions were coming thick and fast now, pain she had never felt surged through her body. The doctor was telling her to push and by God, she was pushing, but nothing was happening. She drifted away and when she came to Johan was standing in a green scrubs next to her.

He was holding her hand and dabbing her forehead with a damp cloth. "Come on, Tori, come on, you can do it," he said to her, squeezing her hand in his. The worry on his face was very badly concealed.

One huge contraction hit her and she pushed with all her might as the first of their babes was born. "Well done, Tori," the doctor said to her. "You have a baby boy, now come on you have two more to deliver before you can all go home," he said to her through his mask. The baby was wrapped up and taken away.

Five p.m. that night she delivered another boy and twenty minutes later a girl. All were very small but healthy and unharmed from their early arrival. Tori lay exhausted in her hospital bed. She was so relieved that they were okay. Johan was looking at the babies through the glass of the premature baby unit. He was filled with such pride and happiness he thought he would burst. Kurt had managed to get hold of him eventually when he had come out of the forest and back to their home. Johan had received eight messages from Fiona and another four from Kurt and had turned his truck round and driven like the demons of hell were behind him. He was terrified that they would not make it, they were small anyway but six weeks premature was just not good for the babies. He had made it to the hospital just in time to see Hans arrive into the world.

Tori was allowed home the following day but the babies had to stay in hospital for a few weeks until the doctors were sure they were okay and up to a decent weight. They had decided on names for their children – Hans for the first son, after Johan's father, Thorren for their second and Agnetha for their beautiful daughter. Tori had not wanted to leave the babies but they told her she could come every day to see them. Johan had driven her home the following day, taking her to see Carlos on the way back.

She had stood inside his stable, leaning against the wall and watching the giant horse eat his dinner. He was spreading a lot of it all over his bed. She wondered how different their lives would be now they had the babies. Her insides felt like she had been hit by a truck and she was weak. She had lost a tremendous amount of blood but she had wanted to come home. She didn't want to stay in hospital, and if she couldn't stay with her babies she would rather be with Johan.

Johan was filling up Carlos' hay nets and came back into the stable to hang them up. "Well, lady, we did it," he said to her as he hung the bulging nets of hay for the hungry horse. "We are now a mum and dad." He turned to her and kissed her with passion. "Tori, I love you beyond all measure," he said to her. "You have made me the proudest and happiest man in the whole world."

She smiled at him. "Well, you had better take me home and make me a cuppa then," she said to him.

Chapter Twenty-Nine

Tim and Liz admired their new nephews and niece through the glass of the hospital window. "Good job, you two," Tim said, shaking Johan's hand and hugging Tori. "How does parenthood suit you both?" he smiled at them.

Liz was still looking through the glass at the new arrivals. "They are absolutely perfect, Tori," she said, wiping a tear from her eye.

"Well, so far with them all still being in here we don't feel like proper parents," Johan told Tim. "As soon as the little scamps come home, then we will be in for the sleepless nights and early morning feeds I expect."

He stood with his hands on his hips and his legs slightly apart, wearing his faded Levis, his old fleece and steel toe capped boots. Tori looked at him and her stomach took a huge lurch. She really wanted him, she wanted him to make passionate love to her, to hold her and tell her that everything was going to be all right, their babies would be home soon and he loved her more than ever. She felt terribly guilty having thoughts like that in the hospital, standing looking at their three beautiful children.

They waved Tim and Liz off from the doorstep of their house in the forest. They had stopped with them for a couple of nights so they could visit to the children. It had been so nice to have them stay, to be able to talk about old times and catch up on what was happening in the old world she used to live in. She felt like she had never lived there now, it felt like a story to her and if she hadn't got the scar on her lip she could almost imagine it hadn't happened at all. Tori had made a fabulous meal the first night they had stopped and they had all drank lots of wine. The second night Tim had treated them all to a meal at Angelo's and champagne to celebrate the arrival of the babies. They had been very generous and had bought lots of gifts with them. Tim had explained that Liz had been unable to control herself every time she had been passing a baby shop. Tori had thanked her for the beautiful outfits she had bought them.

Johan was standing with his huge arm around Tori's shoulders as they waved their visitors off on their way home. Turning to her, he took her in his arms and held her for a very long time. They stood on their doorstep, just holding each other and trying to absorb what had happened in the last week. He knew she was all over the place emotionally but realised she needed to see her brother. She had not seen him in a very long time and they were close. He would have suggested that they visit at a later date if it had been anyone other than Tim on the phone that morning. Still, it had been good for all of them to see each other.

They went inside and he led her upstairs. They were only supposed to be holding each other on their large bed but it turned into a lot more than that. He was so gentle and she felt so loved and secure in his presence. She grasped his vast arms and screamed with her release.

He kissed her on the forehead and rolled from her. "I am sorry, Tori, I know we were not supposed to let that happen for another few weeks. I am really sorry, I hope I didn't hurt you?" he asked, feeling ashamed for not being able to control himself with her.

"No, Johan, I am so glad it happened. I needed to feel you love me still and that you are not cross with me about the babies." He was lying on his side with his head propped on his hand, elbow on his pillow.

"Cross with you, what on earth would I be cross with you about?" he asked, surprised at her statement.

"Because the babies came early, I didn't know that I was pregnant and I have moaned about not being able to do much whilst I was pregnant. I am so sorry, Johan, I have really put you through it the past few months," she finished.

"Tori, you have made me the happiest man alive," he said, stroking the hair away from her face. "Please, don't think things like that. You told me you didn't know, why would I believe anything different? It wasn't your fault the tribe decided to arrive six weeks early and I can't blame you one bit for being frustrated," he said. "All that you did before you were pregnant with Carlos and helping me, you were so

146

independent it is no wonder you felt fed up. God, Tori, you must speak to me if you have feelings like this, not bottle them up inside." He tucked her hair behind her ear and ran his fingers over her cheek and the tiny scar that remained from her fall from Carlos all those months ago.

"I am sorry, Johan," she said, getting up from the bed. "I sometimes worry that I will lose you. You have had a lot to cope with lately: me arriving, us getting together, a damn hard winter this last one, Angus retiring, pregnancy and now three babies about to come home in the next few weeks." He laughed at her.

"I am made of strong stuff, you know. Part Viking I am, and don't forget that, woman," he laughed. "Come on, I will make you some dinner," he said as he bounded down the staircase and into the kitchen.

She ran herself a deep bath and soaked in the bubbles. She was very sore from the birth still but she also felt a whole loved woman now Johan had taken her to bed. She lay in the bath and thought about him. He was crazy. In the last ten months he had changed his life beyond all recognition. Fiona had told her that he had not dated anyone of any significance for years and years. She told her she had held a torch for him but had given up all hope of ever getting a date. Tori wondered what she had that none of the other women did. He had taken on someone twenty years younger than him with baggage and God knows what else and had not batted an eyelid. He had taken her as she was and looked after her, loved her and put up with her moods and irrational behaviour. He was an absolute saint of a man.

Surfacing from her bath, she rinsed the bubbles from her tired body and dried herself on a big fluffy towel. The towel was warm and she stood wrapped in it, savouring the warmth as she sat on the edge of the bath thinking about her lovely man. She applied a large amount of body lotion, rubbing it into her dry skin. She had been very lucky and had regained her shape after the babies had come.

She stroked the lotion into her skin, thanking God she didn't have huge stretch marks or excess skin to cope with. She had always tried to keep in shape and it looked like it had paid off.

She dressed in her pyjamas and pink dressing gown and went down stairs. Johan had poured her a glass of wine and was making vegetarian chilli.

"Sit down, lady," he said to her, "It is just about ready." He pointed to a chair with the wooden spoon in his hand.

She sat down and he served a huge pile of chilli and rice onto her plate. He then put an even larger pile on his own plate. She smiled to herself about his terrible portion control. She would probably only eat half what he had served up for her but she knew he would finish what was left.

The chilli was delicious and so was the wine. It had been so long since she had enjoyed a glass of wine so when she had finished her first one, Johan poured another. When she woke up later that night, she was in bed with him next to her. She must have fallen asleep on the sofa and he had carried her upstairs. She had not done that in a very long time but she was so tired these days she could hardly think straight. She fell straight back to sleep again.

He woke at two am and went down stairs to get himself a glass of water. He sat at the large kitchen table with his glass of water, looking at the pictures of their babies on his phone. They were beautiful children. He felt so very blessed to have three babies and an amazing woman who was mother to them all. He thought of his life a year ago, before he had met her and how lonely he had sometimes been. He remembered the first time he had seen her on Carlos, the day she had fallen off and he had found her. She had passed out at his feet and he had carried her and led Carlos to the roadside before taking her to the hospital in his truck. He remembered his feelings right back then that he had wanted to be with her, he had never felt anything so strong. He remembered the early morning on New Year's Day when they had not been able to control their feelings any further and had made crazy, passionate love on the floor of the cottage lounge in front of the fire.

All these things were running through his head when he looked up and saw her standing in the kitchen in front of him. Her hair was all over the place and she was rubbing the sleep from her eyes.

"What are you doing down here, big man?" she asked him, yawning. "Trying to avoid me or something, are you?" she reached inside the cupboard and took a glass out and ran herself some water.

"No, lady, I am just reflecting on how damn fortunate I have been over the last year and looking at our beautiful creations," he said, turning his phone round to show her the pictures of their children in their cots in the hospital.

Tori sat next to him at the big table and put her hand on his leg.

"I know everything will be all right, Johan," she said, looking at him. "We are a very strong little family and we will come through this very soon," she reassured him.

Stroking his cheek with the back of her hand, she kissed him and led him back to bed.

Chapter Thirty

They stood holding their babies in the hospital.

"They are all doing incredibly well," the nurse said as she handed Hans to Johan. "They should be able to come home in the next week," she continued, handing Agnetha to Tori and holding Thorren herself. "They are absolutely adorable babies," the nurse cooed over them. "Are you prepared to have them back at your home yet?" she asked, looking from one to the other.

"Yes, we have had everything ready for weeks," Johan replied. "The only thing is we have had to buy tinier clothes, the ones we had look massive against them." He looked vast, holding tiny Hans in his arms. Tori looked at them and felt a huge surge of emotion overwhelming her.

She turned away with Agnetha as tears started to run down her cheeks. She was having a hormonal moment, at least that was what she had told Johan they were. He picked up on this and handed Hans back to the nurse. He put his arms around her and their baby daughter and held them.

They were back home and in the nurseries. There was one for the boys and one for Agnetha. The boy's nursery was decorated in beige with blue accents and for their little girl she had yellow and white decor. In each of the rooms was an old rocking chair that had come from Tori's mother's house. Tori and Fiona had made the curtains and cushions for each of the chairs and Fiona had made changing mats and bumpers for the edges of the cots. She had turned out to be an amazing friend to Tori, who was so grateful to her. She had taken her under her wing and introduced her to the important people in the village as she had called them. The vicar, the hardware store man, the publican and head of the women's institute. She had helped Tori master the sewing machine, which was somewhat of a mammoth task for her, and now she and Johan were admiring their handiwork.

"This time next week they will be home," Johan turned to her with a big smile on his face. "Life will never be the same again," he stroked her cheek as he made the comment. "But boy, am I looking forward to it!"

"Life will certainly be very hard for a long time," she replied. "We are going to be very tired for a long time too," she said as she straightened the curtain in the boy's room.

"You and Fiona have made a great job in the nurseries," he said, as he watched her tweaking the pencil pleats on the curtain rail. "I didn't think you were so good on a sewing machine," he added.

"No, I am dire on a sewing machine. It is all Fiona's help and patience that have resulted in all this," she said, indicating the soft furnishings around them.

"Tomorrow, I am planning on a huge wood cutting session in the barn," Johan told her. "I want to try and get a little ahead of myself to allow time for looking after the babies." He stood, looking out of the window down at the barn. "I have enough to last about ten deliveries in there at the moment so I will get it all done before they come home."

The following morning he was good to his word. At six a.m. Tori woke and found he was already outside in the barn, making a start on the wood. She got dressed and made him porridge and toast with a large mug of tea. She called him in for breakfast and he told her he would be out there in the barn for most of the day if he could manage it. He was beginning to realise his limits. Although he loved the satisfaction of cutting the wood up, he also realised his days of spending all day out there were getting limited. He was fifty-three now, and a father, and had to realise his priorities.

After Tori had been to sort Carlos out, she returned and started to load the trailer up with wood. She would be okay if she took it steady and didn't push herself. She managed a couple of hours and then went in to make lunch. Johan made light work of the six ham and cheese sandwiches she had made for him and finished his tea with two slices of fruit cake. She watched him eating and hoped that they would be all right when their family became complete. She hoped that the strain of it would not break them and that Johan would love her as much as he did now.

She cleared away the plates and washed them in the sink before loading up the rest of the trailer. When she had finished the trailer, she found the bags from last winter and started to load them up, stacking them in a corner of the barn. She knew they would be fine financially but she knew Johan felt responsible for keeping the village and beyond warm during the winter. She didn't want him working himself into an early grave as her father had done.

She thought of her father often those days. He had been a wonderful man full of adventure and cheer. The exact opposite to her mother and she had often wondered how their marriage had worked so well. He had worked in stocks and shares like Tim and had made a lot of money but had died of a heart attack way before he retired so he never got to enjoy their money. He had been very good and left both of his children and his wife extremely well provided for. She would not have been able to make her way this far in life on a florist salary, she knew that much. Her memories of her father wandered on as she ironed the tiny baby clothes she had just taken off the washing line outside. She stacked them in boys pile and girls pile. She wanted everything ready for when they came home.

In the kitchen, she unpacked the sterilizer and packs of bottles they had bought. She washed them all and left them to drain. She bought the formula powder, gripe water and all the other medical potions she thought they might need and distributed them between the kitchen downstairs and upstairs bathroom cupboard. She couldn't believe how much stuff three little babies needed. What a good job their house was a decent size. How did people with small houses manage, she thought as she busied herself with all the preparations.

Chapter Thirty-One

The babies were home. One week had passed and Tori and Johan felt their whole world was upside down and running on very slow time. They would finish one baby and another one or two would need attending to. Johan had initially thought he would be able to get a couple of hours work in each day but the first week was a blur. Tori had called James and asked him to look after Carlos for the week at least as it seemed to be one dirty nappy after another and then the bottles and then the washing and so the cycle started again.

The first week Tori felt like she and Johan had barely spoken to each other unless it was to ask for nappies or a bottle to be filled or a fresh baby grow. She felt like she was on a hamster wheel. Johan was starting to feel very stressed. He was trying his best but that didn't seem to be good enough or fast enough to suit each child. He and Tori had survived on beans on toast and easy to make dinners. She didn't like him not having his usual mountain of food and worried.

At the end of week three, Fiona called by to find Tori in a flood of tears.

"Fiona, I cannot manage on my own with everything I have on," she wept into her sleeve. "I feel such a failure. We have brought these three babies into the world and I feel like the worse mother imaginable," she cried, sitting at the kitchen table with her head in her hands.

Fiona stood up and turned the kettle on. She went over to Tori and hugged her tightly.

"Tori, look at what you have been through in the last year. Look at yourself, is it any wonder you are knackered?" she said, looking at her. "Nobody could manage with three tiny babies and all you two do." She made them a pot of tea and put the tin of cake between them both. "Now, I am going to come over tomorrow as it is my Wednesday off. I am going to look after the babies for the morning and you can go and see the other man in your life at the stables – go for a ride even, but you need to get out and have time for you," she said, holding Tori's wrist. "And when you come home I will have made you both some lunch and you can then go out for the afternoon and do some shopping or whatever you want to do," she told her. "You need some time away, you cannot be expected to cope like this," Fiona said, "and I hate to say it but if your mother was here she would have quite possibly come to help you for a few weeks. Well, she isn't, but I am, so each Wednesday for at least the next six I am coming to babysit and help you out." Tori hugged Fiona, she was such a good woman with a kind big heart.

Johan was pleased to hear of the plan. It was now mid-October and he was worried that they would be in for another bad winter like the last one. He had been busy in the forest and the plantation, marking up and grading his trees for selling as well as trying to help with the children. It was taking its toll on him and he was hardly able to keep awake after his dinner at night. He had known it would be hard on them but it would get easier, he had kept telling himself.

One afternoon, when he did manage to finish by six p.m., he came indoors and told Tori he had seen the vicar in the village and had been discussing marriage. She looked up at him from the potatoes she was busy spreading on a cottage pie.

"What marriage?" she asked him. "What have you been talking about?"

He told her that the vicar had known they were engaged and had enquired if they had set a date yet. Johan had told him that he would love to do the deed but didn't know if Tori was ready.

She looked at him in disbelief. "What, you want me to plan a wedding when I am spending all day elbow deep in babies?" she snapped at him. "I can't believe you told him that."

She was cross with him now, he had said too much. "Okay, just forget about it, forget I even mentioned it, Tori," Johan said, standing up and stomping off up the stairs to shower. She sat down at the table and hid her face in her hands and cried.

Did he really want to get married, she thought to herself? She had never felt so tired or unattractive in her whole life and he wanted to marry her looking and feeling like that. Was he mad, she wondered. She pushed the pie into the oven and went upstairs to talk to him.

"Johan, I am sorry, I didn't mean to snap at you," she said as she sat on the lid of the toilet whilst he showered.

Drawing back the shower curtain, he replied, "No, Tori, I don't expect you did mean to snap, but that is all you do at me these days. I can never do anything good enough for you or the children and I am trying my best, you know?" he said back to her, snatching the curtain back around him.

She was shocked by his words. Was this really what she was like, is this what she had turned into over the past few weeks? She didn't know what to say to him so she went back down stairs.

Standing at the Aga with a glass of wine, she looked at the man in front of her. She had changed and so had he, he looked years older than fifty-three and his hair had turned very grey in the last few weeks. She had put him through a tremendous amount in the last year and she felt terrible for it. He looked at her as he pulled his chair out and sat down at the table.

"Johan, I don't want to fight with you," she said softly to him. "I love you. I am so sorry if I have been a bitch, I really am sorry, please believe me I don't want anything bad to happen to us," she told him.

She poured him a glass of wine and put it down in front of him. "Tori, I have tried so hard to be patient with you, to support you and provide for you. You know what it was like here last winter, you know how hard it was and that was when we didn't have three babies to look after," he told her. "I don't know what you expect of me. I know you are tired and missing Carlos and you only have Fiona to help you now Mary has gone back to Tenerife but you are just too much." He pushed his chair back from the table and walked out of the door, closing it behind him.

She was stunned. She took the pie out of the oven, burning herself in the process, and sat at the table and cried again for the second time that evening. She was finding it so hard to cope and she wished she had someone to come and help her, she felt very alone sometimes. She didn't know the first thing about looking after children and she had tried so hard to be a good mother but at the detriment of her relationship with the man she loved more that life itself, the father of those children. The man she did want to marry one day when she felt normal again. Life was so hard at the moment and she couldn't see when it would start to get easier for them.

Tori lay in bed later that night, alone. She didn't know where he was or if he was coming home or not that night. She had cried all night, cried through feeding the babies their bottles and last nappy changes. She had sat on the sofa and cried through a whole bottle of wine. She felt terrible. All the way through their relationship, they had been so very close, she loved him so much and they had had something very special. Now she had blown it because she was tired. She hoped that he would come back but inside she thought that he might not. What would she do if she had blown the relationship? They had never had a row before and she didn't want them to have another one.

Late that night, Johan let himself back into the wooden house. He was feeling very guilty for his outburst. He knew it would have upset her and she was trying her very best to be a good mother and look after him too. He had known when she told him she was pregnant this would not be easy especially when they had found out they were having three babies. He slipped into bed next to her and put his arm around her thin shoulders. She had lost a lot of weight lately, he didn't think she was eating properly and drinking too much, quite possibly. She made a small sound in her sleep and rolled over taking him in her arms she pulled him close to her and she wrapped her leg around him. God, he loved her. No matter how bad things could be, that would never change.

Chapter Thirty-Two

She woke up and realised he was next to her. He had come home. She moved up to him and put her arm around his body. She moved her leg up and down his, very slowly and seductively. She moved towards him and slid her hand down inside his shorts, realising he was awake. He rolled over to face her, reaching for the buttons on her pyjamas. He quickly undid them whilst she removed his shorts. He pulled her pyjama bottoms off in one quick motion and threw them onto the floor. He climbed onto her and she opened her legs fully to allow him in. She wrapped her legs around his waist and pulled him into her, moaning with the pleasure she felt at having him inside. He kissed her all over her neck and breasts, gently caressing them, feeling her rise to his touch. He pushed harder and harder into her and as she dug her short nails into his back, they finished together. He could be a beast in bed when he wanted to be and that night he had been. She loved it when he was like that, it made her want him even more. He kissed her and held her against him until the light of the morning was starting to come through the curtains.

The following morning, Tori had made a life changing decision. Fiona had arrived to look after the children so Tori made her way in her old Volkswagen into the village to the church. There she found the vicar.

"Well good morning, Tori," he greeted her with a big smile. "And how are you and those lovely little babies of yours doing?" he asked, full of concern for them. She thought that Johan must have said something about her struggling.

"We are all very well, thank you, vicar," she replied. "But it is the other thing Johan was talking to you about that I have come to see you over," she said. "The wedding idea."

The vicar's face bloomed into a very big smile. "Yes my dear, yes indeed," he said. "Let me get the book and we can see when there are vacancies." He went off and rummaged around, before returning. "When were you thinking of, Tori?" he asked her, flipping through the pages of his appointment book.

"I don't know, when do you have any spaces?" she asked him.

"How about Christmas day?" he said, looking at her over his spectacles.

"Wow, can you do that for us?" she asked him. "Really, Christmas day, he would love that," she said, feeling excitement.

"Yes, we can do that for you and Johan." The vicar flicked his pen and started to write down their names. Now, she had done it, booked the wedding, and she would need to tell Johan before he found out. She knew what the village grapevine was like.

Back in her old car, she drove to see Carlos and took him out for a ride in the forest. She was hoping to find Johan to tell him the news. He was working on some young trees when she caught up with him.

"Hey, Johan," she shouted across to him so he would put his saw down and not spook Carlos. "I have done something a bit rash this morning," she told him. He held Carlos' rein as she told him what had happened.

Johan was speechless. "I thought you didn't want to get married," he said, looking up at her shading his eyes from the low sun with his hand.

"Yes, I do want to get married to you, Johan. I want you to be my husband and to be Mrs Tori Andersen but I felt overwhelmed by it all with the kiddies," she said, as Carlos stomped his large hoof down onto the forest floor and started to paw the ground, a sign he was getting bored.

"Tori, I don't know what to say," Johan replied to her. "You never cease to amaze me, woman, and you could not have picked a better day. That was the very same day my parents got married in Norway," he told her. "Christmas day!"

She felt so happy. Now she would have to get herself together and sort out the wedding. She called Fiona from the stables to check all was okay with the babies and told her she had something to ask her when she got back. Carlos was back in his winter rugs again. He marched off across the field to see his friends and she returned his head collar to his stable door. She had mucked out his stable and quickly hung his hay net, filled his water and made up his dinner ready for James bringing him in later.

Tori hurried home to break the news to Fiona. She was absolutely delighted for her. "Please let me help you, Tori," she pleaded, holding her hand. "I can do your flowers?" she asked her, "and anything else you will need help with?"

"Fiona, I need help with everything. You know how busy Johan is at this time of the year, I cannot expect him to be able to help me, he is far too snowed under with wood deliveries, plantation care and God alone knows what else he is doing out there all day," she said, hugging an overjoyed Fiona. "I am grateful for all the help I can get and, it isn't going to be that long until Christmas day is upon us and I don't even know where to start looking for a dress." She suddenly thought she was going to have to start relying on Fiona and Kurt an awful lot if this wedding was going to happen.

Tori sat Johan down on the sofa that evening and told him what she had been up to. He took her hand and told her if she was not ready they would wait.

"Johan, I could go on not being ready for the rest of our lives," she told him. "I want to be your wife, the mother of your children and for us to be a proper family," she said. He hugged her and then hugged her again.

"Tori, you never cease to amaze me," he told her.

Tori sat at the table where so much had happened in the last year and made her list. All the things she had to do for the wedding to happen on time. She had decided to make the cake herself. It would be a simple fruit cake plainly iced and only single tier. There would only be around thirty people at the wedding anyway so she didn't see the point of making a huge cake that would probably be wasted. She had made plans with Fiona to go and look at dresses, taking the babies along too. Tori thought that a very adventurous move, but Fiona assured her that it would be okay. She had called Angelo's and they had agreed that she could hire the whole place out for their wedding.

They had been so overjoyed to hear the news that they were getting married and had kindly offered free bottles of champagne for the wedding toast.

She had asked Tim to give her away and he had agreed. Both Tim and Liz had been very surprised to hear that they were getting married so quickly after the babies were born but he knew his sister well and had never seen her so happy. She knew what she was doing, he was sure of that, and Johan was a remarkable man. There would not be many men ready to be a father to triplets at fifty-three, he realised that from the beginning. Fiona had said she would do the flowers and Kurt was going to drive her to the church in his car. He had insisted, so who was she to say no?

The babies were all growing at a great rate. She knew the boys were going to be massive, like their father, and Agnetha was going to be smaller, like herself. She could see so much of Johan in both the boys already. They had settled into a much better routine now and barely woke up at all after their eleven p.m. feed. She was proud of them and proud of how they were forming as a family. She would often take them all out with her to see Carlos. Parking the buggy outside his stable, he was very curious as to what the little wriggling bundles were about when he first met them. He had put his large head over the stable door and very gently had touched them with his long whiskers and had a good sniff. She thought he knew they were only baby humans and was impeccably behaved whenever she took them to visit him.

She had just put the babies to bed, all bathed and smelling of baby smell, and was preparing to make Johan and her dinner. He came in from the dark winter evening. Bringing a gust of the cold in, he quickly closed the door behind him. He took off his coat and hung it on the coat rack next to hers. She always had a little smile to herself when she saw her size twelve jacket against his almost big enough to fit Carlos, she often thought.

"Hey, lady," he said, coming over to kiss her. "What is on the menu for tonight then?"

She opened the fridge and looked inside. "Well, I was going to do you a steak and veggies and I made an apple crumble with the apples from the tree in Mary and Angus's garden if you are up for dessert?" She replied, turning to face him with the crumble in her hand, along with the milk. "So is it cream, custard or ice cream tonight then?" she asked him, holding up the milk carton.

"Damn it, woman," he replied mockingly, slamming his fist on the table. "This is why I will never be slim," he said, running his hands through his hair in pretend shame.

"Yes and as long as I am alive you will be fed properly," she said, placing the milk down on the worktop and getting the custard powder out of the cupboard.

There was not much left out of the huge glass bowl of crumble. Tori had not eaten any and Johan had only left a tiny portion that she told him was not worth leaving. She scraped it into his bowl and poured the remaining custard onto the top.

"Come on now, lady," he said, picking his spoon up and tucking in. "Do you want me to get into that wedding suit on Christmas day or not?" He said, between mouthfuls of crumble.

"You are no heavier than you were a year ago, Johan. You have to realise you have a very physical job and it is getting cold outside now, so you need to eat well and keep up your strength."

He did as he was told and finished the crumble. She took the bowl from him and washed it up, along with the other dishes. Standing at the sink with her yellow rubber gloves on, he realised how much she meant to him, how she had changed his life for the better and how he was so much longing to have her as his wife in a few weeks' time.

Chapter Thirty-Three

The days were short and the nights were long. The Herefordshire winter had arrived again in the forest. Johan was busy with his plantation, getting trees harvested and netted and delivered out to the various shops and customers who were wanting them at the end of November. He was grateful for when Tori could help him with his deliveries. She could manage most days if she put the babies into their seats in the back of the truck and timed the deliveries between feeds. She would try and time it so she could be home for feeding and nappies and then go out again with more wood later on that day. It was far from ideal, but they managed. She never got the deliveries done quickly though, as everyone wanted to come and see the children. People had been so kind to them and the old ladies had been busy with their knitting needles making tiny outfits for them.

Thank goodness Johan had cut up so much wood all that time when the babies had been very small. Now they had a good pile to use for delivering. Tori knew it wouldn't last all winter but there was enough for now, she thought. She would quite often take a couple of Christmas trees out to customers who had requested them along with their wood delivery. She often thought of the day when her tree had turned up unannounced on the doorstep of the cottage and she had wondered who had left it for her. That lovely Nordman was now planted at their house. Tori had wanted to keep it so badly as a memento of their first Christmas together and had not allowed it to go back to the plantation. Tori planned to decorate the little tree with some lights when it got closer to Christmas, she planned to do this every year from now on. She would never forget that tree, she had told Johan she wanted to look at it every day when she left and returned to the house so it was planted outside by the door. Johan hoped that it would survive there.

Days spent with Carlos happened mostly at weekends now when Johan could look after the babies or they took them down with them.

Tori didn't run anymore, she couldn't spare the time even to run to the stables. She realised that it would not be any time in the next few years that she would be able to do another desert ultra-marathon. She didn't mind.

Tori had been living in Herefordshire for over a year now. It seemed hard to believe that over a year had passed since she first rode the bridleway in the forest. She had ridden it so many times in the year since, her most favourite route. Her life prior to her move seemed so far away now it was hard to think that only one year had passed.

Tim and Liz had been down a few times to see them all. They stopped at their house and they had all enjoyed the time spent together. Tim took Tori down to see Carlos, he couldn't believe what a relationship she and this huge horse had together. This horse had been so nervous and skittish he had not wanted to take him on. If he had been smaller he would have kept him as a companion pony but he was 17.1 hands high. Tori had instantly fallen in love with him the first time she had seen him and Tim had to admit Carlos had been a changed horse after she had spent only a week with him. This had made Tim's decision to give her the horse for her twenty-first birthday present. As he stood before him now, it was an incredible transformation.

Liz had been more than happy to look after the children. They had not ever been able to have any of their own, which had devastated their mother when they had broken the news to her. That is possibly why she had put so much pressure on Tori to stay with Nick and have children. She had wanted to be a grandma so badly. It was a pity that she and Tori had not had a better relationship, she thought as she watched Liz with the babies. Her mother would have had three grandchildren in one go to look after and coo over.

Tim and Liz had left with the promise they would be down to help out prior to the wedding. All things were going ahead, Tori had made the cake and iced it. It was safely in the kitchen cupboard, hidden away from Johan's hungry hands. Fiona and Tori had decided on the flowers and they had spent an afternoon in town trying on wedding dresses.

Fiona had cried almost all afternoon at every dress Tori had tried on until she told her off.

"Come on, Fiona, you are supposed to be helping me choose, not crying at every one I come out in," she had complained.

Choosing wedding dresses had not been Tori's favourite task and she wanted to be able to get one there and then. They had been limited due to the time scale of the wedding being only in a few weeks. The consultant had pulled a long face when Tori had relayed this information and informed her.

"You will have a very limited amount of dresses to choose from then, we really need at least ten months' notice." Ten months, Tori thought, ten months' notice! I had hardly known Johan then, let alone considered marrying him. Stupid woman, she had thought to herself.

The dress had been chosen and paid for that day and Tori had left it with Fiona for her to look after. Thank goodness it hadn't needed to be altered as the woman in the shop had told her that would be another three weeks. Did these people live in the real world, Tori had wondered?

Fiona and Kurt had taken Johan to buy his suit. Angus had agreed to fly back with Mary to be the best man and he already had a new suit, he would wear that. Johan was marched off to town and the suit was bought. That was in the wardrobe in their house.

Tori ticked all these things off her list and put it away in the drawer.

Johan walked in from his work. She looked up and her stomach did a little flip. All these months they had been together and her stomach still flipped and her heart still beat hard in her chest when she saw him.

She sent him upstairs to shower whilst she put the babies to bed. Bottles drank and nappies changed, they were all settled into their nurseries when he appeared in the doorway.

"Can I do anything to help?" he asked her, rubbing his hair on a towel.

"No, they are all sleeping now, thank God," she said, leaning over Thorren's cot. "I think they might be starting teething, they have all been a nightmare today," she said, looking at the beautiful child now asleep in the cot.

He walked over to her and put his arms around her waist as she stood facing the cot.

"We will deal with it, Tori, you know we will," he assured her.

She turned and kissed him putting her arms around his neck.

"Come on, big man, let's get you fed and watered." She led him downstairs and into the kitchen.

Chapter Thirty-Four

Tim and Liz had arrived on the Wednesday, the day before Christmas Eve. Tori had been in Fiona's shop, going through the final flower ideas. Two arrangements for the pedestals in the church, her bouquet, two button holes and two corsages. They were red roses mixed with eucalyptus and, of course, small branches of Nordman fir. There would be a massive Christmas tree and candles in the church and Tori hoped more than ever that the heating would be on.

It snowed, just like it had the previous year. It was thick and fluffy underfoot and terrible to drive in. It had taken Tim three hours to get there in his 4x4 but now they had arrived.

Johan was cutting up more piles of wood in the barn, leaving Tori and Fiona in charge of arrangements, he had told Tim. "You know what women are like with that type of thing," he had said, leaning on the log splitter.

Tim had rolled up his sleeves and helped Johan all afternoon with the wood. By five thirty p.m. they had a huge pile ready for bagging up and loading into the truck. Liz had spent the afternoon inside with the children. She and Fiona were going to be looking after them on the wedding day and she was so excited. She adored her nephews and niece.

Tori arrived back at the house. She was very excited that Tim and Liz were staying with them. Climbing out of the Volkswagen, she hugged them both. "I am so pleased you are here, I am sorry the weather is so bad, hope the journey wasn't too crappy?" she said, with an arm around both of them.

They went inside where Johan was poking the fire into life. Their little family were all lined up in their bouncing chairs, waiting for their feed.

"Just give me a minute and I will get the kettle on, just need to feed the scamps," he said, piling formula into three bottles on the side.

"No tea tonight, Tori," Johan announced, standing up from the now roaring fire. "We are getting married in less than forty eight hours; we are having champagne!" he went to the fridge and pulled out a bottle.

"Angus gave me this earlier when he came over to see how we were getting on." He popped the cork and they all cheered. "A toast!" Johan announced, following her into the lounge with the third bottle, "To my soon to be wife," he said, raising his glass and the feeding bottle.

Tim and Liz raised their glasses and Tori raised the two bottles in her hands. "Thanks, Johan," she said. "Now, can you feed Hans if I do Thorren and Agnetha?" she asked.

"No problem, lady," he answered, putting his glass down, picking up the tiny child and putting the bottle into his gawping mouth.

Tori had made a large pasta dish for them and they all sat at the kitchen table, eating and drinking the champagne Johan had produced. They all chatted loudly with one another. There was much laughter and the mood was good.

"This one is from Mr Smith at the hardware shop in the village," Johan had told them as he stood at the sink and popped the cork on the second bottle of champagne. Bubbles had gushed out of the top of the bottle and into the sink as he tried to pour the liquid into glasses.

Tim had asked if he could go down to see Carlos with her in the morning and asked if Liz could look after the children. Tori had said that would be a huge help if she didn't mind, she had seating plans and the cake to drop off at Angelo's. Also to sort out her dress at Fiona's house and then come back and help Johan. Johan had told her that Angus had said he would come and help him pack up and stack wood and do the final delivery before the wedding so she didn't have to.

The following morning, Tim drove her to the stables. Inside Carlos's stable, he asked her if she was really sure this was what she wanted. Rug in her arms, she turned and faced him.

"Tim, I want this man more than anything," she said, looking him in the eyes as she replied.

"But, Tori, your life here is so hard, just seeing you the last couple of times we have been down here you are always working. You have three kiddies to look after and this big chap here," he indicated to Carlos, who was waiting for his turn out rug to be put on. "I just hope you have thought all this through and are sure it is what you want," he finished.

"I have thought this through, Tim, and Johan is the man I want to spend the rest of my life with. He is the father of my children for God's sake, he rescued me from a very bad and dark place, Tim; you didn't see what happened here last year. If Johan hadn't been here I quite possibly wouldn't be either." She threw Carlos' rug over his broad back and fastened the front, belly and leg straps without looking at Tim.

She fastened Carlos' head collar around his head and lead him out to the field. "I know life is hard here, Tim, but I would rather have a damn hard life here with him than an easy life without him".

Tim understood. He just had to be sure. He liked Johan a lot but he had secret concerns; the man was twenty years older than his sister and the work was so physical he didn't know if she would be up to it for the long term.

Tim parked his large 4x4 next to Johan's. Tori went inside the house and fetched her seating plans and the cake carefully stored in an airtight box. She put them in Johan's truck and went into the barn to find him. Angus was alongside him, stacking wood in the bags and piling it all up at the back of the barn

"Hi Angus, lovely to see you," she said, giving him a big hug and kiss. "Hope Mary is okay and not too cold in the house? I did turn the heating on a week before we knew you would be back," she added.

"Good to see you, Tori," Angus hugged her back. "You know we would not miss this wedding for the world," he said, standing back from her. "But we have to get this wood sorted out so you guys can have a little break for a few days."

It had already been decided. Between Angus, Mary, Fiona, Tim and Liz they had booked two nights away for them whilst a joint effort was going to be taking place looking after the three babies. Tori had tried to argue but they would not hear anything other than her saying yes to the arrangement.

Tori told them she was just running the cake and seating plans down to the restaurant and would be back soon. Climbing into the pickup, she started the engine and drove off down the track. Angelo's was buzzing when she arrived. It seemed like every member of staff had turned out to help prepare for the wedding the following day. She walked in and everyone cheered and came over to speak to her. It was over two hours later, when she had finally seen all the place settings, the cake stand and table and sampled the champagne that she actually managed to get back into the truck and drive home to collect her things.

That evening, Johan stayed at home with their children and Tori stopped at Fiona and Kurt's house in the village. Tim and Liz were with Johan. They would be fine, she had convinced herself. Tori lay awake most of that night in the single bed in Fiona's spare room. She stared at the floral wallpaper the little room was decorated in, very aware of the great commitment she was about to make the following day. She felt very nervous but didn't know why. She had never been so sure of anything in her life. This was the man she wanted to spend the rest of her life with. She couldn't imagine her life without him now. She tossed and turned all night and woke the following morning to more snow on the ground.

Chapter Thirty-Five

The morning was very cold. It was Christmas day, their wedding day. Tori stood in Fiona's shower, letting the hot water rinse away the conditioner in her long blonde hair. She let the hot water surge over her slender body, enjoying the warmth of it. She dried herself and then her long hair with the hairdryer she rarely used. Fiona knocked on the door and then entered the room with a breakfast tray containing a glass of Bucks Fizz.

"Hello soon to be, Mrs Andersen," Fiona chirped at her. "How are you feeling on this cold Christmas morning?" she asked, sitting beside Tori on the bed.

Tori finished drying her hair and put the dryer down on the floor. "Nervous, Fiona, I feel so nervous I don't think I can even eat that delicious breakfast you have so kindly made me."

Fiona put her arm around her shoulders. "Come along, you need to eat, it will be a long time between photos and the wedding breakfast, you know, and I don't want you fading away mid-afternoon," she joked.

Tori smiled and picked up a piece of toast. "I know, sorry, Fiona you are right as always," she said, chewing on the toast. "I will eat this up and come down to join you when I have got dressed," she replied. "I suppose I need to start putting my wedding dress on around lunch time?" she asked her. "Are the flowers all okay, have you been into the shop to check them?" she asked looking worried.

"There is no need to go into the shop and check them, Tori, you know we left them in water yesterday in the cold shop. The flowers are in the church ready and they will be fine, I gave them plenty of water after the service last night so you don't have to worry about anything," she said, getting up and taking the tray away with her.

Tori had already spoken to Liz earlier that day about the babies and she had told her everything was good back at their home. Johan had not been able to sleep that night either. She had heard him pacing around most of the night in his room. Maybe it was because they were away from each other Tori had thought, she hoped they would never spend another night away from each other in their whole lives. She missed him and their children.

She sat drinking tea at Fiona's dining table. "Come on, Tori, you need to get yourself dressed. Time is starting to get the better of us." Fiona was flapping, holding up Tori's wedding dress to take upstairs to the bedroom. "Have you brought everything you need with you, are you absolutely sure you have not forgotten anything?" Fiona clucked around like a mother hen.

"No, Fiona, I have got everything. I have done my hair and make-up and all that remains is to get into the dress and put my tiara on. Now, why don't you go to the shop and pick up the flowers so Kurt can take the button holes to the church and be ready for Johan and Angus?" she suggested to the panicking florist.

"Yes, you are right, I will go and pick them up now and get Kurt to take them up to the church and then come back for you," she said, wringing her hands.

Johan was fixing his tie in the long mirror in their bedroom. Stepping back, he looked at his reflection. He had never been so dressed up in his life and that alone made him feel nervous. He wondered how Tori was feeling that day, wondered if she too was nervous. He thought she would be and resisted the temptation to call her. He wanted to hear her voice, to be reassured. Looking on his phone, he read through the messages of good luck he had received from his friends and customers. He felt overwhelmed by it all. He turned his phone off and put it into his jacket pocket. Taking one final look at himself, he went downstairs to load the babies into their car seats.

Tori stood in Fiona's lounge in her wedding dress. Fiona had cried again when she saw her standing in all her splendour. She looked beautiful and Fiona knew Johan's heart would melt when he set eyes on his bride. Her dress had been a sample from the shop in town, a silk sheath dress with a lace overlay. It was so simple but elegant and chic.

It flowed to the floor, just covering Tori's shoes. She had a simple tiara in her hair, which she had styled herself into an 'up do'. She wore diamond earrings and the necklace Johan had given her one year ago to the day. She touched the necklace and felt the pendant. How much had changed in their lives since that day one year ago. She wore the engagement ring he had given her on her ring finger, which is where it would stay until the day she died. In her hands she held a small bouquet of red roses and eucalyptus tied with a red ribbon.

"Are you ready?" Kurt said, as he walked to the door. "Your carriage awaits." He opened the door and helped her down the steps to his car.

Johan stood at the altar, looking down at his hands. He was so nervous. The church was full of friends and clients who had come along to wish them both well.

Angus stood at his side and offered him a drink from his hip flask "No thanks, Angus, I don't want to be fumbling my words. But thanks for the offer," he told him, patting him on the back.

"You have got the rings with you, haven't you?" he asked. Angus reached into his pocket and opened his hand to reveal the two rose gold wedding bands they had chosen.

"Thanks, Angus. Sorry, I am just so damn nervous," he said, rubbing his hands together. It was cold in the church even though the heating was cranked as high as it would go he could feel the chill in the air.

A moment or two later, Tori had arrived at the church. The congregation stood up as the bridal march started on the huge church organ. In she walked, with Tim at her side, proudly walking his sister towards her future husband. Johan's breath was completely taken away when he saw her, she looked stunning.

He stood with his mouth open, staring at this amazing woman who was about to agree to be his wife. "You look amazing, Tori, totally mind blowing," he whispered to her as she arrived at the altar. "I love you so much, lady." He turned and smiled at her and she smiled back, squeezing his hand. In his entire life, he had never pictured this moment and as he looked at her by his side, a small tear escaped the corner of his eye.

The ceremony was very emotional. The vicar had been so pleased to marry them both and had spent a lot of time with them discussing what they would like including in their ceremony. The hymns Johan had chosen which had been favourites of his church-going parents. Tori cried through her vows. Most of the guests cried too. Liz and Fiona sat together, sharing a pack of tissues and bouncing the babies on their knees. There was not a sound from any of them.

The vicar pronounced them man and wife and Johan kissed her like she had never been kissed before. He had such passion and energy she felt she would faint in his arms. The congregation stood up and all cheered very loudly. Turning to face their friends, they walked out of the church together… Mr and Mrs Andersen… into the fading light of that Christmas day afternoon and into the cold snow outside.

Later that evening as they danced their first dance, pressed closely against each other, she whispered into his ear, "Johan, I love you more than life, you have made me the happiest woman in the world. You have made me your wife and the mother of the three most gorgeous children and for that I will never be able to thank you enough." She put her arms around his neck and kissed his clean shaven cheek. "And you have actually had a shave for the first time since I have known you," she laughed.

After their guests had left later that night, they drove to the Lake District and spent the night in a five star hotel in Windermere. They were so tired they fell into bed and didn't wake until late the following morning. Ordering room service, they sat in bed eating breakfast.

Johan was getting crumbs all over the bed sheets and she was trying to brush them off. "Johan, this is a five star hotel, you know, not our house, you can't make a mess everywhere with your toast like you do at home," she playfully scolded him.

Taking the toast out of his mouth, he lifted the tray and put it onto the bedside table before he pulled her down into the bed.

"No, it might not be home, but this bed is much more comfortable than ours so I think we should test it, don't you think so?" he said as he pulled her pyjamas over her head and threw them onto the floor, "Come on, we are married now, lady, it is okay for us to do it and make a lot of noise too," he announced as he took his shorts off and threw them on top of her pyjamas.

As always, she couldn't and didn't want to say no to him. They didn't get out of bed until lunch time that day, after consummating their marriage. In the afternoon they took a walk along the winding paths around Lake Windermere. It was cold and blowy but they were well wrapped up in cold weather clothes.

Returning to the hotel late in the afternoon, they sat in the bar and drank whisky together. The log fire was roaring in the hearth so they sat with their chairs pulled up, talking about the last year in their lives. They talked about their children and called home to see all was okay there. Tim answered the phone and said they were all okay and Liz was loving it. Tim had been down to see Carlos that day and he was all right too, they were not to worry and he would see them tomorrow evening when they got back.

They ate a large dinner that night. Johan tucked into a massive steak and she had vegetarian risotto. They ate Christmas pudding for dessert, with heaps of brandy cream, and then had another glass of whisky before leaving the bar and retiring to bed. The past few days seemed to have gone by in a blur. The wedding had gone so well, they were sitting in bed and looking at pictures that people had forwarded to them of the day's events on his phone. They looked so very happy together.

She lay in bed with his head on her lap. She was stroking his hair when she realised it was the anniversary of Nick's accident, the day he had beaten her so badly. Her stomach did a flip inside as she touched the scar still very visible on her bottom lip.

He looked up at her from his book. "I haven't forgotten, Tori," he said, looking at her upside down. "I know it is a year today since Nick's accident and what he did to you, I just didn't feel it was the right time to bring it up so I left it to you. I figured you would talk to me about it if you wanted to," he finished.

She looked down at him, still running her fingers through his hair. "I know, it is never a good time to think about it, but it happened. Maybe if it hadn't happened we wouldn't be here now."

"We would be here now, Tori," Johan said, sitting up. "We most definitely would be here now." He turned to face her. "I knew when I saw you that very first time, riding Carlos through the forest, I knew I wanted you and once I had met you there was no way I wasn't going to have you, unless you didn't want me," he told her, propped on one elbow on the bed.

"You know I wanted you, Johan, the demons I was wrestling with were if you were rebound, that haunted me for ages... well until New Year's day morning, when I realised you were not rebound," she laughed, and ruffled his hair with her hand, making it stand on end.

"Yeah, that was a damn good way to celebrate the arrival of the New Year, wasn't it?" he smiled, remembering their night of unbridled passion. "I think we should try and replicate that night tonight." He grabbed her ankle and pulled her down the bed. "Now."

Chapter Thirty-Six

They arrived back home late the day after Boxing Day. Tim and Liz had already gone home, leaving Fiona in charge of the babies. Tori walked into the house with her bag and put it down, heading straight for the lounge where Fiona and the children were.

"Fiona, I am so glad to see you, has everything been all right here?" she asked, picking Thorren up out of his baby bouncer and kissing his little pink cheek.

"Yes, all has been okay, just teething issues keeping them awake at night but I have given them all some medicine so you should have a relatively quiet night tonight," she said, showing Tori the teething gel. "I am going to get off now if you are okay here?" she said, getting up from the sofa and collecting her coat.

"Yes,, that is fine, thank you so much for everything you have done for us, Fiona. We are so grateful and have had a lovely couple of days away," she smiled, hugging Fiona as she left, still holding Thorren against her.

Johan kissed Fiona and thanked her as she walked past him to her car. "Well that is it then, Mrs Andersen, looks like we are a proper married couple now with responsibilities," he said, kissing Thorren and then her. "Let me loose with the other two scamps," he said, picking up Hans and handing him to Tori so he could reach Agnetha.

That night the babies didn't sleep. They were up all night with teething problems. Tori was glad that they had spent the last day or two relaxing and could face a sleepless night. She left Johan to sleep, not much woke him up and he needed the rest. He had been looking ill in the run up to the wedding, even Angus had said as much to her. She worried about him.

The following morning she was up early, preparing the bottles for the babies when he came bounding down the stairs

"You sleep well?" he asked her, kissing her cheek, reaching mugs out of the cupboard as she did so.

"No, not really, the children were up most of the night teething," she replied, screwing the tops on the bottles and shaking them to mix the formula.

"God, Tori, I am so sorry, I didn't even hear them crying," he said. "I was out like a light last night and don't even remember you getting up at all."

"That's probably because I only got up once and didn't get back into bed. It wasn't worth it because once one was happy at least another one wasn't," she smiled at him, testing the temperature of the bottles on her wrist. "Will you start breakfast whilst I go and feed them?" she asked him, pointing to the porridge in the saucepan.

"No, I am coming to help you and then we will do breakfast together. You know I am rubbish at porridge at the best of times and babies come first," he said, wiggling a finger at her and taking the third bottle out of her hand.

Johan was back out in the barn, cutting up and sawing more wood. Angus and Mary had gone back to Tenerife and Tori was alone in the house with the children. She had just finished a huge pile of washing and was setting the iron up for another huge pile. Babies did seem to generate an awful amount of washing and ironing. All the children were asleep upstairs in their beds and she was making the most of it.

Fiona had been round that morning and told her she was thinking about selling the shop. Fiona's parents were elderly and didn't live in the area, she was an only child and was thinking about moving back to Norfolk to look after her parents with Kurt. Tori hadn't known what to say. Fiona was a woman with a very good kind heart and she had a good relationship with her parents which helped. They also had a very large house so she could live in part of the house with Kurt. Tori admired her. She had become very close friends with Fiona over the last year and she didn't want her to go, but she also sympathised with her and understood she had to do the best thing.

"Do you really have to sell the shop though, Fiona?' she asked her. "Couldn't you rent it out so you could come back if you wanted to?" she enquired.

Fiona explained that she would not come back. She wanted to sell the florist and use the money as her nest egg for when she and Kurt bought a house together which was what they planned.

Tori thought about their conversation as she ironed the baby grows, folding them into neat piles. She had thought about buying the florist shop at one stage but that had been before she had found out she was having three babies. It would be too much now she couldn't manage a shop and three children, plus helping Johan out with the wood and her dear Carlos. She had wanted to take up floristry again, it was something she had loved doing, but now was not the right time in her life. She also didn't want Fiona to leave. She was a friend and in some respects a mother figure to Tori. She had looked after her and sometimes been the voice of reason when Tori had been over emotional and needed to hear a few home truths. She didn't want to imagine what it would be like without her but it looked like she was going to have to.

She finished the clothes and put them all away in the cupboards in the nurseries and her and Johan's room.

Making her way quietly down the stairs, she planned to start baking next. Taking out her cookery books, she perused them to see what she hadn't made in a while. The tins were empty and Johan did like his massive hunks of cake every day, sometimes twice and on the occasion she had not been around to monitor him, three times a day. She didn't mind, she wanted to please him and make him happy. Smiling to herself, she thought of the day she had caught him with his third piece of cake. She got the ingredients out of the cupboards.

An hour later, she was taking golden flapjack out of the oven. Wearing Johan's old oven gloves, she placed them on the worktop to cool. Cutting it into large pieces, she carefully removed the warm oat delight from the tin with a cake slice and put it onto the wire cooling racks. She made a fruit cake, carefully mixing the fruit into the mixture she filled the tin and put it into the already hot oven. There, she thought, that would last him a few days at least!

Chapter Thirty-Seven

The 'For Sale' sign on Fiona's shop had now been replaced with a 'Sold' sign. Tori had helped Fiona pack all her possessions into the van she had hired to take her and Kurt to Norfolk to live with her elderly parents. It was a sad day for Tori, she was losing a friend but, as Fiona had told her, she was only at the end of the phone if she needed her.

It had been a great surprise to Tori and Johan when Liz had called from Leicester to tell them she wanted to buy Fiona's florist shop. She and Tim had spoken and they wanted to move closer to their niece and nephews. Liz missed them terribly and wanted to become a bigger part of their lives. Tori had been overjoyed at the news but what about their house, she had asked. Tim had been on the lookout for a similar property in the surrounding area and although what they had found was smaller, they no longer needed so many bedrooms as they wouldn't be having children or their mother to stay with them. The house they had put an offer in on was still enormous. Tori and Johan had looked at each other in amazement as they were shown around the four bedroom equestrian set up they hoped to buy.

Liz had tentatively asked if she could help out with the children more, so would be freeing up Tori to help Johan. She was also very aware Tori needed her time with Carlos and that wasn't happening at the moment. Liz had horses and she understood the time spent with them was and escape from the everyday world. On the days Liz didn't help out with the children, she was going to be running the florist shop, although not working there herself, she explained. It was all sounding perfect.

Tori and Johan kissed Fiona and Kurt and closed the van door. Tori was choked up as they waved them off into the distance. As soon as they were out of sight, she cried into Johan's chest; what would she do without her dear friend? Johan, as always, comforted his wife. He too was sad to see his friends leave the village, it was the end of an era for him.

Tim and Liz would be moving down in a couple of weeks if everything went to plan. They had sold their huge house very quickly and had put all their things into storage. They always stopped with Tori and Johan when they came to Herefordshire, Tori was always so excited when they came to stay and had almost burst with joy when they had told her of their plan.

"There is no need for us to stop in Leicestershire now Mother has gone," Tim had explained to her one night. "I can commute from Herefordshire as easily as Leicester, you are my only relative now, Tori, and your family is our family, so we want to come and live closer to you all," he had told her one night when they had been down with them.

Tim and Liz left for Leicestershire later that afternoon. Tori went down to see to Carlos. Tim had already offered Carlos a stable at their new place but she had wanted to keep him close by and at the stables he was at with James at hand to help out. She was standing, looking over his door, when James came over to see her.

"Your brother is moving down here then?" he asked her as he stood, watching the huge horse eat his hay. "What has made him move?"

Tori told him the story, she told him everything that had happened over the past year with Nick and Johan and the passing of her mother and how good Tim and Liz had always been and the fact that they couldn't have children and had wanted to help out with theirs sealed the deal. Tori told him she was sad Fiona had to leave, that they had been really good friends, but it was good that her brother would be here.

"He is moving into that place with the indoor and outdoor school, isn't he, does he have horses?" James was fishing, probably thinking that Tori was going to leave the yard.

"Yes, he does have three horses, and he has asked me if I want to move Carlos over there and I have declined his kind offer," she said, smiling at James. "I really appreciate everything you have done for us over the past year, James, and I know I can trust and rely on you to do things my way, so I am not moving." She touched his hand and he hugged her hard.

"That is exactly what I wanted to hear, Tori Andersen." He hugged her again. They had become very good friends and she was a little bit pleased that he had been worried she might move away.

Tori got home and decided to go out for a run. She had not been running in absolutely ages and needed the air and her own space. Johan was bathing the babies and putting them to bed so she changed into her gear, tied on her trainers and turned on the head torch. Outside, it was getting cold but she ran and ran, covering eight miles of forest tracks. She arrived back home, puffing and panting like and old train and covered in dirt, but she started to feel like their life was going to get back to some sort of reality.

She thought about the desert marathons. The company she had raced with all those years ago still had her on the mailing list and every few months an email would come through telling her what was going to be their next event. She knew she couldn't even contemplate racing yet, not until the children were older, but a time would come she thought to herself.

That night, she went into the spare bedroom and carefully rummaged around under the bed. Dragging out a crate and an old cardboard box, she found all her old racing kit out. She sat on the edge of the bed and went through it all piece by piece. Her backpack, sleeping bag and mat, her first aid kit, still mostly intact, and her race outfit. It would never look new. She had realised that after spending a week racing in the same top and shorts. On her return she had soaked it all in a bucket for three days and washed it twice but the dirt was ingrained into the kit. Part of the experience, she had thought to herself at the time. She had everything she needed to do the event, she wouldn't need to buy anything too expensive to do the event, only to pay the entry and flights to wherever she was to decide to race. She packed it all back up into the crate and box it had lived in for the past two years and put it back under the bed. She would keep the race as a goal, something to aim for in the next couple of years, she thought to herself.

Chapter Thirty-Eight

Tim and Liz had moved into their new house, five miles away from Tori and Johan. It was great. They went over regularly and Liz would cook for them and they would eat in their grand dining room. Liz did like the fine things in life, Tim had explained to Johan one day, hence why the house had to be decorated in the most expensive wallpaper and the fabrics for the curtains were the most exclusive. Johan had raised his eyebrows and silently thanked God that Tori wasn't that way inclined. She had not changed anything about their house after she had moved in, only the flowery duvet cover that had become a huge joke between them. When she had ironed it, she would send him upstairs to put it away only to find he would hide it so she couldn't put it on the bed and would resolve to put one of his checked ones on instead. He had told her that his house is her house and she was to do whatever she wanted regarding changing the décor, but she hadn't wanted to change anything, only the duvet cover. Once the babies had arrived, they had to decorate the nurseries but that had been it. She had loved the house the way it was and that had secretly pleased him.

Liz would visit and help them out with the children, usually two or sometimes three days a week, which had been a great help. On those days Tori would help Johan with his wood deliveries first and foremost, or if Johan was working on the plantation and didn't need her around she would go and ride Carlos. They would go out on long rides through the forest, trying to find new tracks and bridle ways to follow. Or sometimes they would go off up towards the Malvern Hills, when James could ride with her.

He had lived in the area all of his life and knew every bridle way, so if he was off on a ride he thought she would enjoy or had not been on before he would invite her along. They would go off for hours at a time, enjoying the fresh air and the cold winter wind on their faces.

She would always return feeling like the old Tori again and happy she had spent time with Carlos.

Johan had tried to work part time as he had planned but he had been stuck with the wood deliveries. He had been told he was not going to get anyone to help him, so he had stopped working in the forest all together and spent all his time either on the plantation or cutting up wood. He thanked God that Tori delivered the wood for him. Having Liz help out was brilliant for both of them. On days when Tori didn't ride, she would go out for a long run, usually in the forest, then return and take the pickup and trailer out. She was used to it now and got the deliveries done quickly most of the time.

It was one of these days when Tori had been out riding Carlos with James in the morning and was doing the wood deliveries in the village that afternoon. She was unloading three bags for Mr Smith at the hardware shop, her last drop of the day, when Mr Smith caught her.

"Tori, do you have a minute?" he asked her, "I have got something I want you to see." He led her through to his back room and showed her a small dog, curled in a basket by his fire.

"Do you know anyone who would like him?" he asked her. "He was found wandering around the village. He is not micro chipped and nobody knows who he belongs to or where he came from. He just appeared one day and I really can't have a dog when I am in the shop all day, it is not fair on the little chap. He is really good with the kids though, when the grandchildren come by they take him out to play with them," Mr Smith added.

She looked down at the little dog wagging his stump of a tail at her. "Johan will probably kill me," she said, scooping the little dog up in her arms. "And if he does I will send him straight to you," she said, wiggling her finger at Mr Smith, "but I will take him and see how he gets on with forest life."

She bundled the little dog into the back seat of the truck, complete with his basket, and set off back home, wondering how she was going to explain herself to her husband this time.

She opened the door of their house with her free hand still holding the shivering dog in her arms. "Johan, are you here, where are you, big man?" she asked, struggling with the basket Mr Smith had insisted went with the dog. "Johan, are you upstairs?" she shouted louder. He was, he was putting the children to bed, he shouted down to her from the landing. She sat at the kitchen table, holding the little dog to warm him up inside her coat, wondering what his reaction would be.

Johan appeared, his large frame filling the doorway carrying three baby bottles and a towel over his arm. She looked up at him from her seat at the table and opened her coat.

The little dog peeped out from his position on her knee. "Aah, where did you get this little chap from?" Johan asked, coming over to stroke the dog, a big smile on his face. "You are so sweet little chap, is it a chap or a girl?" Johan asked, looking at Tori for confirmation.

"Yes, it is a chap, and Mr Smith has been calling him Basil," she said, placing the dog into Johan's open arms. "You are not cross with me?" she asked him as she removed her jacket and hung it up next to his.

"Cross with you? Why would I be cross with you? I have wanted a dog for years but the opportunity never arose. Now, we have our little family it is the perfect time to get one."

He put Basil down on the floor, where he started to examine his new surroundings. "I think it is a brilliant idea, he can come out with me during the day on most days. We do have a very much outdoor based life, Tori, so he will fit in great."

She was relieved he had taken to Basil so well. "Mr Smith gave me a pile of dog food that is in the truck so I'll just go and fetch it inside. Basil gets fed about six so I'll do it in a minute and then start dinner." Tori went back out to the pickup and took out the dog bowls and tins of food Mr Smith had given her. Carefully juggling it, she went back inside and started to make room in the cupboards.

"Right, Johan," she said, moving around tins of beans and spaghetti. "This is going to be the dog cupboard so anything food, medicine or grooming dog wise is to go in here." She stood and pointed out a cupboard that she had cleared.

She made dinner for them and they sat at the large table enjoying a huge plate of chicken balti, naan bread and rice and Tori made herself a vegetarian version. Basil sat at their feet, looking hopeful. Johan reached down and fussed the little dog.

"You don't want to eat balti, Basil," he told the dog, "you will have a very upset tummy if you do. This isn't dog food, little chap." Basil moved away and sat with his head on his paws, looking dejected.

They sat together on the sofa, drinking tea. Johan reached into his jeans pocket and pulled out a piece of paper. Unfolding it, he handed it to her. "Here, Tori, thought you might like this."

She looked at the sheet which had flight details on it. "What is it?" she asked, looking up at him.

"Read it, lady," he replied. She looked down and read the flight schedule. "It's to Chile?"

"Yes, to the Atacama desert, a place I seem to remember you saying you would like to go back to one day." She looked at him and then back at the piece of paper. "But what about the children?"

"They are stopping here with me," he replied. "You need to have a break, Tori, you have not stopped since you moved here, you have been to hell and back and then had three kids, now it is my turn to send you on a sort of holiday." He put his arm around her shoulders, she was speechless. The race was the following week.

"I don't know if I am ready for this," she told him.

"Yes you are, you have trained and trained and trained and if you are not ready now you never will be."

"Oh my God, I cannot believe I am going back next week," she screeched, jumping up from the sofa and waving the piece of paper with her flight on around in excitement. "I can't believe it!"

He had known she had been in the room and looked at her old race kit. He had seen on her laptop the race details the organisers kept sending through to her and Tim had told him of her love of the races and her desire to never give up on the idea she would do another one someday. She had never mentioned it to Johan after the children were conceived, probably because she thought she would never be able to race again. He had enlisted the help of Tim to get him the details and Liz had helped him book the flights. Now she was going next week and he was seeing a different woman in front of him.

Chapter Thirty-Nine

There was so much to sort out. Liz had offered to come over and look after the children for the ten days Tori would be away racing and travelling. Johan had cut enough wood to enable him to only deliver in the mornings whilst she was away and he would have the children in the afternoon and evenings. It had all been arranged. The race entry fee had been paid and so had the flights. She was to fly from the UK to Madrid onto Santiago and then Calama, doing the return flights over a week later.

Tori dragged her kit out and checked everything again. She made spread sheets with her calorie intake on and dragged Johan off to Sainsbury's to buy her race food, which was mainly noodles and anything easy to transport, vegetarian and with a high calorie content. She was so excited but worried about leaving Johan and the children behind. How had he known she wanted to go again? She had never said anything to him once she had found out she was pregnant, racing was to be a thing to be considered in a couple of years or so, when the children were older. He was such a good husband to her.

James was to look after Carlos; he had been asked before Johan had even considered booking the race. If James hadn't been available to look after her horse, then she would not have even considered going. She stood, stroking his long muscular neck and feeding him treats. She would miss him. Chile wasn't like going back to Leicester, it was two days travelling, more or less, and she wouldn't be able to get back in a moment's notice from the desert. They would have to find where she was on the race field and then pick her up and bring her back to the airport, if they would even do that for her. She hoped he would be okay with James. Johan had promised to call the race organisers if anything was to happen to him.

She had everything packed and repacked, pulled out and packed again to make sure she could fit everything she needed into her pack.

She trained around the forest with it on, something she should have been doing months ago, really, but she knew she would be all right carrying the weight, she had done it many times before.

The night before she was due to leave, she lay in bed with her husband by her side. "Johan, you will all be okay without me, won't you?" she said, turning to face him in the darkness.

"Of course we will be all right, Tori, but that doesn't mean I am not going to damn well miss you, lady." He turned onto his side and put his arm around her, pulling her close to him. "I am counting the days already to when I get to that airport to pick you up." He kissed her forehead in the darkness of their room.

"Don't think I want you to be away from us because I really don't, but I also understand these races are a huge part of your life, Tori, and you need to do them to keep you sane. You need to be out there, training and pushing yourself, so you can come back here to all this and be you and not some crazy woman." He stroked her cheek with his hand.

She leaned up and kissed him on the lips. He pulled her over on top of him and pulled her pyjamas off. "So let's make up for the next ten days when we are going to be away from each other," he said, removing his shorts with one swift movement.

Whatever happened between them in their everyday lives, whatever type of day they had or how tired they were, the sex was always brilliant between them.

Tori rolled off him and went into the bathroom in the dark. Johan lay in bed, wondering how he was going to manage for ten days without this woman by his side and in his bed. His life would be like it was before she had come along. He knew the babies would keep him busy, but he wanted her.

Very early the following morning, Tori was eating breakfast at the table. Liz had just arrived and Johan was outside, warming up the pickup truck. All her gear was in two bags by the door – her race pack and a small case which contained things she was not worried about losing or had to go into the hold. All her vital equipment that she would not be able to race without was in her pack.

Finishing her toast, she stood up and drained the last of her tea. She put her mug into the sink and walked over to her kit. Collecting it all up, she took it outside to the truck.

"Don't know why you wouldn't let me put it in for you," Johan complained from inside. "It is damn heavy you know?"

"Yes, Johan, I do know, I have been running around the forest with this weight for the last week or so and I will have to carry it around the Atacama desert for another week, so I do know how heavy it is thanks." She pinched his cheek. "I am just going to kiss the babies goodbye and I will be out, if you are ready?" He was.

She kissed each child on the cheek and said a silent prayer for them to be kept safe whilst she was away. She hugged and kissed Liz and thanked her for her kindness and then got into the truck. Johan drove her to the airport and stood whilst she checked in her bag, making sure she never lost sight of the one with her kit in, that was to go as hand luggage.

Her flight came up on the board, it was time to go. She picked up her pack and turned to her husband. Holding him tightly in her arms, she kissed him. "Johan, promise me you will call the race organisers if *anything* happens, *anything*, you promise me?" she said, stroking his bristly cheek with the back of her hand.

"Yes, Tori, I promise." He kissed her and watched her walk away, with her pack swinging from her shoulder. He didn't see her silent tears rolling down her cheeks. She would miss him.

The flights were long. She managed some sleep on the overnight flight from Madrid to Santiago and then had a very long wait at Santiago for most of the day. She texted Johan to let him know she had arrived there safely and only one more flight and a taxi ride to the middle of the Atacama where her overnight hotel was. She was already missing him... her man.

The following morning Tori was up early with her race pack all ready for kit inspection, which was scheduled for after breakfast. After inspection by the organisers, the competitors were loaded onto the coaches in the hotel car park to be taken to their first overnight camp deep in the Atacama Desert. Tori was not at all nervous. She had done a few of these races before, she had prepared and trained hard over the past months and now she was ready to start. She introduced herself to the seven men who were to share her tent for the next six days. She would like to have had the company of another woman but hadn't expected it. These races were very male dominated and on a previous race she had been the only woman in the tent. It didn't bother her at all, she would find a woman out on the course if she felt lonely for girl chat. It was going to be hard, she thought to herself as she unpacked her evening rations and tucked into noodles and dried mashed potato.

Chapter Forty

Tori found the first day hard. It was very hot and her pack was heavy but when she couldn't run she walked and so the miles of that first day were ticked off, checkpoint by checkpoint. She was not allowed contact back home during the race, so when she had eaten her evening meal and tended to her sore feet, she looked at the photos she had brought along of Johan and the children. She missed them very much, she felt a deep sorrow inside her that she had to come and do the race but she knew she would be better once she was back home again.

The second day saw two of Tori's tent mates pull out of the race. One was so badly dehydrated he was on a drip in the medical tent all night and the other one had severely twisted his ankle on a rocky pass they had to negotiate. Tori had raced very hard that day. She had seen on the route map that there would be several river crossings. She didn't want to be slow through them, leaving her at the back of the field, she would find it very hard to make up the time in the afternoon when it got hot again. She ran as much as she could through the morning when it was cooler and finished in the top third of the field. She was pleased with herself but also very aware that she must not push herself too hard so early in the event.

Day three, Tori was getting a fed up of noodles and dried mashed potato. She had found in previous races that was the best food for her to obtain energy and palatability. Some of the previous pre-packed food she had tried had not been appealing after day two and she had not been able to eat it leaving her compromised. She mostly grazed throughout the day on food she kept in her front pack, which was usually sweets.

Johan's eyes had almost fallen out of his head when he had seen the bags of sweets she had packed in with her food rations. "Big man, I need to have instant energy and eating sweets is the best way for me," she had told him, trying to explain herself.

He had laughed and told her she would come back three sizes larger if she ate them all. She smiled to herself, remembering that day as she walked through the vast and tremendously beautiful Atacama Desert on that Tuesday afternoon in February. When she returned to her tent that night, she discovered a couple of blisters had appeared. Not surprising really, she had covered seventy miles in three days over mostly sand and despite her best preventative measures, some sand would get into her trainers and cause friction. She popped the blisters and dressed them, hoping that they would not be too problematic in the next day or so. She retrieved her painkillers out of her first aid kit and put them into her front pack, thinking she would probably need them tomorrow if the blisters started to hurt.

The race was very challenging. She had met a couple of people as she sat and ate her evening meal around the camp fire who had four people in their tent who had pulled out on day three. It seemed that most people were just not taking on enough fluids and electrolytes. Tori knew from previous races that you had to keep these up so your body would function. If you didn't you could at worse, suffer death. On her first race, back many years ago now, she remembered a runner had died. She had been really shocked when it had happened and could only think of the poor man's family back home and how they must have felt hearing the news.

Tori awoke on day four to another of her tent mate telling her that he couldn't do another days racing. She had thought he would finish the race so she spent the first two hours of the day trying to persuade him to continue.

"Come on, Jon, you know you can finish if you just take the maximum that you can on painkillers and just keep putting one foot in front of the other. You will finish."

"Tori, I just don't have your focus, I cannot keep going and going despite the pain in my feet and the blisters on my back where my pack has been rubbing," he told her. "And I am fed up with spending so much of the race alone, it is so lonely out there." Jon had a tear running down his tanned, rugged face and he quickly wiped it away, thinking Tori had not seen it, but she had.

She moved her pack closer to his and sat on her rolled up sleeping bag to eat her breakfast. "Come on, Jon, don't tell me you have come all this way to go home without that medal? All those months training you have done. Think how you will feel when you get back home."

He looked over at her. "I know, I know how I will feel, I have raised $10,000 in sponsorship and I will be letting all those people down," He couldn't hold the tears back and they just overflowed down his cheeks.

"Look, Jon, I will walk with you today. Give me your noodles and I will get the hot water for you whilst you pack your bag up, I have just about finished my breakfast and my next job was collecting my water so I will pick yours up too, give me your card." She held out her hand and he handed her his card. This had to be punched every time water was handed out so the race directors would keep stock of how much water was being consumed. Jon thanked her, feeling pathetic against such a strong woman. He thought she would leave him half way through the day and he would have to pull out anyway.

Tori and Jon walked the whole stage together. She kept him upbeat and also made sure he took his pain medication to ensure his feet were not too bad. They arrived back at the camp that night in much better spirits. Tori told him to go back to the tent and sort himself out. She would collect their water and bring it over for them. She felt having Jon to look after was a distraction from missing Johan and the children. She was finding that by focusing on Jon and getting him to the end of the race she was helping someone and making a new friend too.

Day five was the long stage of the race. Tori was racing fifty miles through day five and into day six, depending when she finished. She decided to adopt the same strategy as she always did. She packed all her day items into her front pack and packed a small plastic bag into a side pocket that would contain her head torch and a spare along with batteries, gloves and night time hat. It got very cold in the desert at night. This way, when she stopped at the checkpoint she got to before dark, she would take her pack off and swap over the day items for night ones, ensuring she could carry on throughout the night with little bother.

Tori asked Jon if he was joining her for this long and torturous stage of the race, to which he readily agreed. They set off at seven a.m. on that Thursday morning. They were both evenly matched pace wise and ran a few miles and then walked into the afternoon when the temperature hit forty-two degrees, then started to run in the evening when it cooled until the terrain got too rough and they walked again. They stopped at each checkpoint along the way to fill up with water and ensure that they took their medication.

Tori's feet were very painful now but she made sure she dressed them properly every morning and left the dressings off overnight so they could dry and air. This was all new to Jon so Tori was more than happy to show him the ropes and lend her first aid kit to help him. He had come quite ill prepared, but so had she on her first race. She told him, experience is a great thing and he would know all this for his next race she had told him. Jon had not been so keen and told her once that race was finished he would not be taking part in another one. He told her on day four if she hadn't helped him he would certainly have pulled out. He had hit an all-time low but now, thanks to her, he had bounced back a little at least. She knew that would be enough to get him to the finish line unless injury stopped them.

They raced through the night and into the following morning when they caught sight of the camp as it was getting light. They were cheered by the organisers as they crossed the finish line, happy and exhausted. They hugged each other, laughing that they had only the short day of six miles left to finish. Tori could almost taste the medal, but she would never tempt fate.

They ate a large meal and lay in their sleeping bags, trying to get to sleep. It was hard because people kept coming into the camp and others would cheer them so they only really managed to nap. Jon was asleep for most of the day so Tori woke him late afternoon and told him he needed to eat and take on more fluid as well as his painkillers. Jon said a silent prayer to thank God for sending Tori on that race with him. He knew he would not have finished if it hadn't been for her kindness and support. He was so grateful to her for what she had done.

Day six, and they were side by side on the start line. Everyone was running the last six miles today, so they had eaten what was left of their food and were ready to take on the final stage. Two river crossings and they could see the village where they would finish. Tori sped up, making Jon struggle to keep up with her, but he did manage. They ran through the village with almost empty packs bouncing around on their backs. They passed spectators who were cheering them on which made them even faster. They turned up a wide uphill road and could see the finish line. Tori turned and held her hand out for Jon who took it. They ran and ran up that hill and over the finish line. Jon burst into tears but Tori couldn't stop beaming all over her very brown and slimmer face. They were awarded their medals and hugged each other before posing for photos.

Chapter Forty-One

The race was over. Tori was at the airport in Santiago, waiting for her connecting flight back to Madrid. Jon had gone back to Canada earlier that day, promising to stay in touch. He had been very sentimental at the awards dinner the night previously and had asked the organisers if he could say a few words. He had stood up and thanked her for all that she had done, told everyone how she had supported him and helped him with his medical needs and walked with him to get him though his dark days to finishing. Tori had been overwhelmed by his actions. She had wanted to see him finish and in her mind she did what anyone would do for any other competitor on the field.

She was exhausted and her feet were not good. She had very bad blisters but at least she had looked after them and they were not infected. She could feel them throbbing through her shoes that had been done up very loosely before boarding her flight back to Madrid. She knew the next week she would still be dressing them and taking her medication. Races did take it out of her physically and mentally but it was a small price to pay in reality, she thought.

Tori had called Johan when she had finished the race, sending him a picture of her and Jon at the finish line with their medals on smiles all over their faces. She had relayed the whole week to him in about ten minutes, she was excited and also relieved that the race was over and she had finished it. She had hoped that she would finish but she never wanted to presume. There had been races in the past she had not managed to finish and they had destroyed a lot of her confidence. This race had been very tough but worth all the training she had put in. Jon had gone back to Canada and raised over $15,000 on his last count, he told her as they said goodbye at the airport in Santiago. She had been so pleased that he had finished and raised all that money for charity. To her, that was what racing was about.

Tori fell asleep without realising that she had. She woke up when the plane hit turbulence and was shaking around somewhat. Looking down at her watch, she realised she needed to top up her medication and have a drink. She would be in Madrid in a couple more hours and then she could call Johan again. She couldn't wait to be back with him.

Later that day, she had collected her luggage and was walking through to arrivals at Heathrow airport when she saw him, her man. She dropped her bag and ran to him, throwing her arms around his neck.

He lifted her off the ground and swung her around in his arms kissing her face and neck. "Tori, have I missed you?" he told her. "Don't leave me again to go trotting off across the desert with another guy!" he said, laughing and running his fingers through her hair.

"Your hair is so much lighter, it is almost white," he said in amazement, looking at her locks in his fingers.

"Yes, well that is what happens when it is exposed to extreme sunlight," she said, collecting her bag from where she had dropped it.

"How is everybody, who has the babies?" she asked him.

"Said infants are with aunty and uncle back home. Didn't think it would be a good idea to bring them in case your flight got delayed." He took her bag from her and offered to carry her pack.

"It is fine, there isn't much in it now anyway," she said, pulling it over her right shoulder and following him out of the airport to the truck.

He told her everything that had been happening since she had been gone. The children had been fine and Liz had been coping without too much difficulty, although she had said to him that she didn't know how Tori managed with all of them to look after. Tim had decided to work more from home. He had realised that work was not everything and he wanted to spend more time with Liz and his horses. Everyone in Great Diameade had been asking about her and wanting a progress report. He had even received phone calls wanting to know how Tori was getting on in the desert. His wood deliveries had taken so much longer as he had been following her progress on the organisers' website he had to relay everything to every one of his customers. In the end he had given them all the website and her race number so they could follow her themselves. He told her she was a local celebrity and they wanted her to go down to the pub in the next week and tell everyone about it.

Carlos had been very good for James but on the odd day Johan had been down to get him in from the field, he had decided that he would not be caught. Johan had to call James and ask him to fetch him in when he got back from his afternoons off. Johan had told her Carlos thought it was a wonderful game and Johan had chased him around the field for over an hour before admitting defeat and going back home. Not even a pocket full of treats had worked, he told her.

Arriving back at their beautiful wooden house in the forest, Tori unloaded her kit and took it straight into the kitchen for washing. Walking into the lounge, she was greeted by Fiona, who was on babysitting duties.

"Fiona, I didn't know you were back, how long are you here for?" Tori asked, tottering over to hug her dear friend. "Johan, why didn't you tell me Fiona was back?" she said to him as he appeared in the doorway.

"I told you aunty and uncle were babysitting. I didn't tell you which aunty and uncle though. Who wants tea?" Johan departed to the kitchen to make tea for them all whilst Fiona explained herself.

"Kurt and I have decided that we want to move back here," she said, bouncing Hans on her knee. "Living with my parents wasn't the best idea really and whilst it was nice to have money in the bank, I really did miss my floristry work. I called Johan whilst you were away and Liz answered. She told me that she hasn't really done anything with the florist since she bought it so I can either lease it and see how things go, or buy it back."

Tori was amazed, such a turn – around in such a short time. "What happened with your parents then, Fiona?" Fiona explained that they had decided to sell up their huge house and move into sheltered housing, using the money they had left for holidays for as long as they were able to continue to take them.

Tori was overjoyed. "So where are you going to live then?" Fiona was going to be renting one of the cottages where Tori stayed when she first moved to Herefordshire. It was all working out brilliantly, Tori was happier than she had ever been in her life. Her dear brother Tim and his wife were now close by and her best friend and her boyfriend were returning to the village. Not to mention, of course, her amazing husband and three children who she couldn't put down.

Later that night, everyone had gone home and the children were in their beds fast asleep and looking beautiful, she had thought as she looked in on them after her shower. Tori and Johan were in the kitchen with a glass of wine each. Tori was sitting on the edge of the kitchen table, swinging her legs beneath her with her glass and he was finishing putting the pots away.

"Johan, you know I missed you so much when I was away," she looked over at him.

"Not as much as I missed you, lady," he replied.

"I know I will have to continue racing, it is something that is in my blood, but I don't know how I am going to cope being away from you all. I feel so lucky to have everyone around us now that Fiona and Kurt are back in the village."

He put his massive arms around her and kissed the top of her head. "Well, it is all right going off on these missions, Tori Andersen, but now I think it is time that you made up for all that time you have been away from me." He playfully flicked her with the end of the dish cloth.

She grabbed it and pulled him towards her. He put his hands onto her shoulders and pulled her dressing gown down over her arms. She was naked underneath. He started kissing her neck and moved down her body to her stomach. She lay back on the table and opened her legs to let him inside. He was very hard and pushed her up the table as he entered her. Grasping her thighs, he pulled her back to him. Neither of them lasted long and it ended in a frenzy of passion and muffled screams from her. He pulled his shorts back on and blew her a kiss. She fancied him so much as he stood there with messy hair and grey stubble on his cheeks. She realised she loved him more than life itself.

Chapter Forty-Two

The following day it was raining. The children had slept in quite late and Tori had not woken up at all during the night. She usually woke every night after a race thinking that she was still out in the desert and having to make her way to the next checkpoint. She slept soundly and only woke when Johan brought up a breakfast tray along with Basil.

"Basil and I are doing some jobs on the plantation this morning if that is okay with you?" Tori told him she would be busy with the children and that they had arranged for everyone to come over for a get together to look at Tori's photos. She would be busy sorting them out later too, she told him.

Tori wandered around the village shop later that afternoon, loading her trolley with buffet food for later. Everyone to arrive around seven p.m. would mean the children would be in bed hopefully and they could all sit and relax and eat 'beige' food as she called it. She had made some sandwiches, a trifle and quiche that morning and had decided to pop to the village and pick up a few crisps, bread sticks and dips. She had decided she was going straight over to see Carlos after the shop visit, she had missed him so much during the race and had hoped that he had not got into mischief whilst she had been away.

Loading the children into their car seats in the old Volkswagen didn't leave much room for the bags of food. She managed to force them into the foot well of the front seat. She pulled up at the stables and got the children out of the car and into their buggy. Carlos was in his stable, eating his hay, and whinnied to her when he saw her coming down the drive. She parked the buggy outside and went into his stable. She spent an hour grooming him and giving his tail and mane a trim. She loved Carlos so much, he was such a good natured horse. Even though he had given Johan the run around, he never behaved like that with her. She patted his huge golden neck and handed him treats before leaving him for home.

The children were bathed and in bed. Agnetha had been very lively and didn't want to go to bed. It had taken Tori ages to settle her but eventually she was asleep. The boys were much less trouble and fell asleep most nights straight away, just like their father. She was amazed how much both of them were like Johan in every way. She looked down into their cots at them and hoped they would find much love and happiness in their lives. She hoped they would find someone who would love them and make them happy like Johan had made her. She kissed the tip of her index finger and touched each of their faces.

Tim and Liz arrived, followed shortly by Fiona and Kurt. Tori was so glad they were all together again. These people made her so happy in life. They all sat together in the lounge eating quiche, crisps and heaps of trifle as Tori gave them a running narrative on the race photos. She took them through her arrival in the Atacama Desert, showing photos of her hotel, then onto the tent and her tent mates as she affectionately referred to them. Tori went through each day and what it had held in store, to the end, where there was the picture of Jon and her smiling into the camera and sporting their well-earned medals.

"Well I say, good on you, Tori," Tim exclaimed at the end of the photos. "When is the next one scheduled for?" he asked her, smiling and holding his wine glass to her for filling up.

"Don't know, Tim, will have to see." She took his glass and filled it from the bottle in the fridge, thinking about the race next year Jon had invited her on. She walked back into the lounge with the bottle and filled the glass, handing it to Tim.

Thinking there was no time like the present, she blurted out, "Actually, Jon has got a place on a race in Alaska next year. The charity he supported has asked if I would like to go along too," she looked over at Johan to gauge his reaction.

"What have you said to him?" he asked her.

"I said I would speak to you and see," she replied.

"Do you want to go then?" He looked up at her from the sofa.

"Yes, of course I do. Racing is in my blood, I have realised now it keeps me sane but I am also very aware I have great responsibilities here at home and you all come first." She took her seat next to him on the sofa, kissed his cheek and patted his knee. The conversation was closed for now.

Everyone had gone home. The evening had been a fabulous one, everyone chatting and getting along so well they had not gone home until after midnight. Tori and Johan were in the kitchen, clearing the food away.

"Tori, if you want to race you must continue to do it you know," he said, taking her arm and pulling her round to look at him. "You told me so long ago now that you wanted to race and to do so for as long as you could. Why do you think I entered you for Chile? Because I knew you needed something and now I know it was that." She looked at him, into his deep blue eyes, stroking his bristly cheek and hugging him.

"I really understand you know, especially now we have just had over a day back together you are your old self again. It wasn't your fault that we ended up with three beautiful children, I don't expect you to look after them single handed. You need a break, so please, call Jon and tell him you will go to Alaska with him next year, please?"

"I will call him in the morning," Tori replied.

Epilogue

The old lady with the grey hair neatly, arranged into a bun slowly closed the leather bound album with a big sigh. Memories had been flooding her head all afternoon. Looking down at the cover of the book she said, "You see, your grandfather and I didn't really have a very easy time of it in our first year together. It was very difficult for us, but here we are, almost forty years later."

She looked up from the album over her spectacles and into her granddaughter's tear stained face

"Ingrid, my darling, if you feel you need to be with Brad, you must go and be with him." She patted the bed next to her, indicating for the young woman to sit down. "I have been so lucky with your grandfather, he has been such a kind and understanding man. He would have moved heaven and earth for me and he did, allowing me to continue with racing after your mum and uncles were born." She wiped a tear from the young woman's cheek. "Canada is only a day away, you know, you can get flights there and back all the time these days."

The girl replied, "I know, Gran, but I will miss everyone if I leave here. I will miss Mum and Dad and you and Granddad. Do you promise to get them to come and visit me once I am settled?" Her face looked hopeful.

"Ingrid, you know they will come and visit you, they won't need me asking them." She wiped a tear away from her granddaughter's cheek. "Jon said he would go with Brad to meet you at the airport."

She smiled to herself, thinking if she would ever have thought the man she helped in the Atacama all those years ago would be the father to the man Ingrid wanted to spend the rest of her life with. It was indeed a small world.

She couldn't help but see so many similarities between Ingrid's life and her own. She too had fallen for an older man. She hoped that she would follow her heart – it had certainly made her so happy over the last forty years.

The old lady reached into her apron pocket and pulled out and an envelope. "Your granddad and I decided that we would like to give you this just in case there is ever a time when you are away and you need to come back home for whatever reason." Ingrid opened the envelope; it contained a cheque for £5,000.

"Grandma, thank you so much, thank you. I will go to Canada and now I will have this to come home with if I ever need to or decide I don't want to be there anymore. Thank you so much." Her tears were replaced with smiles as Ingrid put the cheque into her jeans pocket.

Tori got up from the bed and walked over to the window. On the other side of the large Christmas tree outside, she could see her husband Johan was fetching wood in for their Aga. She looked down at him and smiled and he waved up to her.

"Come on then, Ingrid, let's go downstairs and tell everyone what you have decided to do."